LEGACY OF AN OUTLAW (THE PEACEKEEPER)

"Poston's [Jason] Peares walks into trouble at every turn. He's tough, quick with a gun, and understanding of the underdog."

—Steven Havill, author of *Privileged to Kill*

"A fast-moving story of guns and gunfighters, with a climactic cattle stampede of Texas-caliber proportions."

—Elmer Kelton, author of *Cloudy in the West*

"An exciting, page-turning traditional western sure to please. Fine work."

—Norman Zollinger, author of *Rage in Chupadera*

"Poston's stylishly written action yarn will generate a strong following among western fans."

—Wes Lukowsky, American Library Association

COURAGE

"Jeffrey Poston understands the craft of constructing his novel and does a wonderful job balancing narrative elements with his dialogue. When his protagonist handles his firearms, you know the author has done his research in describing the action."

—Phillip Hardy, Lulu.com review

A MAN CALLED TROUBLE

"In his first novel, Jeffrey A. Poston has numbered himself among the best writers of westerns working today."

—Biblio.com review Praise for Jeffrey Poston

WARRIORS

"It doesn't get any more real than this."

—D. Brock, Silver City, NM

BOOKS BY JEFFREY POSTON

ACTION/ADVENTURE THRILLERS

American Terrorist: Where is the Girl?
Contagion: American Terrorist 2
Escalate! American Terrorist 3
American Terrorist Trilogy

Joshua Experiment (Call Sign: Raven Book 1)
The End of Everything (Call Sign: Raven Book 2)
The Queen (Call Sign: Raven Book 3)

JASON PEARES HISTORICAL WESTERNS

Courage (Book 1)
Legacy of an Outlaw (Book 2)
Warriors (Book 3)
Manhunter (Book 4)

COURAGE

A Jason Peares Historical Western

JEFFREY POSTON

LOMAS & TURNER PRESS

Editing by The Pro Book Editor
Cover design by Deanna Dionne
Interior design by IAPS.rocks

eBook ISBN: 978-0-9916194-2-9
paperback ISBN: 978-0-9863328-3-8

    1. Main category—Fiction/Westerns
    2. Other category—Fiction/Action and Adventure
First Edition

CHAPTER I

"**J**ASON PEARES!"

Jason pulled back on the reins to stop his horse. He looked over to his left, at the young gunfighter who'd called to him.

The kid flexed his left hand by the gun holstered on his hip. He looked to be hardly more than fourteen or fifteen. Probably hadn't even started shaving yet. The young gunfighter swept his shoulder-length blond hair aside with his right hand and gazed at Jason with excited sky-blue eyes.

Jason took a deep breath and considered his misfortune. He hadn't been in town half a minute and already trouble stared him in the face. No one should have known who he was or that he was riding in.

Jason hadn't even known this town existed until he'd topped the last hill a ways back. Yet he could not deny the gunfighter stood there waiting for him, and the youngster had addressed him by name. He spoke menacingly to the young man.

"You want something, kid?"

"He's waiting for you." The kid nodded up the street. "At the saloon."

Jason followed the young man's gaze up the street. "And who might he be?"

"Mr. Sanderville, the Pinkerton detective. He said for you to join him for a drink. After that, I think he means to kill you."

Jason nodded and looked up the wide dirt path serving as the town's only street. In the few seconds since the kid gunfighter had hollered his name, the townsfolk had vacated the street. A dozen clapboard buildings lined each side of the dirt path. The saloon sat near the far end of town, past a gauntlet of false-fronted shacks. Beyond the town to the north and south, several horse corrals and cattle pens dotted the sparse landscape. With Pinkerton detectives on his trail, the smartest thing he could do was turn and ride out as fast as possible. He gently pulled the reins and turned his horse back to the east. Then he froze.

Two men in black outfits sat on horseback in the middle of the road about a quarter-mile distant. Both held rifles, barrels pointed skyward.

For a second, Jason thought about reaching for his Winchester, but he quickly abandoned that course of action. He knew Pinkerton detectives were expert marksmen. They would take him out of his saddle with their first shots before he got his rifle clear of its scabbard.

Jason reined his horse back around and spoke grimly to the kid gunfighter. "Well, I reckon I ought to oblige Mr. Sanderville with a visit." He nodded to the youngster. "Sorry about being rude to you, kid."

"You thought I was calling you out, didn't you?"

"I thought you were looking to get killed today."

"I can take you," the young man said quickly. "If you're still alive when this is all over, maybe I'll prove it."

"If I'm still alive after throwing down against Pinkerton frontier lawmen, I'd rethink that strategy if I were you." Jason kicked his horse into a walk.

After a few seconds, the gunfighter shouted after him, "I can take you, Jason Peares!"

Jason just waved without turning and continued up the street. The high-noon sun was so bright he couldn't clearly see the people hiding in the darkness of open doorways or the shaded spaces between shacks. He saw only shadows of movement. Frightened townsfolk or Pinkerton detectives? With his reins in his left hand, he kept his right hand close to his holstered gun.

Somehow, the Pinkerton National Detective Agency had tracked him over hundreds of miles, probably for months. They laid a perfect trap to capture him in a dusty place called Franklin Town in the middle of Kansas. Knowing their diligence like he did, Jason figured they had warned everyone to stay off the street when he rode in.

Only two weeks past, Jason had collected his wages in Kansas City at the end of a three month cattle drive. He'd left his crew behind with the excuse of an errand to run just so he could meander alone for a while. At times, he enjoyed having company on the trail, but he quickly tired of the presence of others and always found a reason to separate himself.

He wasn't sure why he preferred to be alone. People always seemed to need to get somewhere, while he found solace in the journey rather than any particular destination. He'd tried to figure it out a time or two, usually on one of his solitary rides after a cattle run. In the end, he just accepted that being alone was simply a part of him, like his hair, his nose, or his gun. It was how he felt most comfortable.

His return route should have taken him back across Kansas, south through the Indian Territory—Oklahoma, he recalled people were now calling it—and down deep into Texas. There he planned to rejoin his outfit and help round up and brand more strays. Unless he could think up a miracle, now his trail would end in Franklin Town.

He rode past the blacksmith's shed and a small stable on his right, then he passed the closed sheriff's office and the tiny hotel on the left. He heard a commotion in the hotel doorway and stopped his horse, poised to confront a threat.

Two women rushed through the door, dressed up very prettily with expensive hats and handbags to match their exotic ruffled dresses. The one on the left had curly black hair and most of her enormous bosom swelled out of her low-cut blue dress. She carried an ornate umbrella to shield her pale skin from the sun.

The woman whispered something to her petite companion, but the slender woman continued to stare at Jason. She even took a step forward, but her companion grabbed her arm. She pulled away from her companion's grasp and ran out into the street, holding up the front of her dress to keep from tripping. She stopped a couple of paces from his horse. For a moment, she stared at him without speaking.

Jason knew what the woman saw as she studied him. He sat tall in the saddle—not a big man, not small. He was fairly ordinary, thin yet muscular, and he had light brown skin. His hair was black and mostly wavy, a bit curly. His piercing brown eyes could be friendly at times or intimidating, depending on his mood.

Jason wore normal range clothes, a simple shirt and pants, same as any other cowboy. A dirt-colored, flat-brimmed Stetson shaded his eyes from the sun. The only thing that distinguished him from any other cowboy was his two-holster gun belt and the two additional guns he wore tucked into his belt, butts facing outward for the easy grab.

"Monsieur," the woman said.

It wasn't a statement, nor was it a question. With only a single word her voice became music to his ears, intoxicating in its husky richness. Her tone was more of a plea for help.

"Mademoiselle," Jason returned in her language. He tipped his hat, then glanced around, wondering what a beautiful, French-speaking woman was doing out in the middle of Kansas. "Can I help you?"

"My name is Renée-Simone Fouché. That's my friend Bonnie Drake," she added, nodding toward the woman on the board-walk.

"You're a Frenchwoman," he said in English.

She nodded. "Can we talk for a moment?"

"Afraid not, ma'am," Jason said. "I've got to attend to a fellow that wants to see me."

"Perhaps after that?" Her voice pleaded with him, and she held his gaze. She seemed desperate, vulnerable.

"Perhaps," he replied. "But I'm fixin' to go up against Pinkerton detectives. I can't honestly say there's a chance in hell I'll live long enough to see you again." He smiled. "But you might just be the most beautiful woman I've ever laid eyes on." And the last, he thought to himself.

Jason tipped his hat again and rode over to the saloon three buildings away. As he dismounted, he watched Renée-Simone rejoin her companion on the boardwalk and slowly walk toward the saloon. In the distance beyond them, the two Pinkerton detectives waited on their horses.

Shame, he thought. He was mildly curious about the needs of the Frenchwoman. His predicament was grim, though. He had detectives behind him, cutting off his escape, and likely there were more watching the other trails leading out of town. No doubt detectives watched him from within the town also, though they were probably staying out of sight until the shooting started. He had ridden into a Pinkerton trap he could now neither avoid nor escape.

CHAPTER 2

Jason Peares had heard a lot about Pinkerton detectives. Back East, especially in the big cities, the Pinkertons had a reputation in years past as gun-toting, hired thugs who wore badges. They were often hired by wealthy company owners to bust up union strikes.

Jason knew the frontier Pinkertons were more accurately described as cowboy detectives. Most were well-educated, very thorough hunters. They were professional in the extreme rather than just rough-riding gunfighters. For frontier work, the Pinkerton Agency recruited only the best trackers, hunters, riders, and marksmen.

In particular, Jason knew of Sanderville's reputation. An extremely resourceful and accomplished manhunter, he was given to civilized treatment of his captives—especially the more notorious outlaws—when lynch mob mentality might otherwise prevail.

Jason considered his limited options. The Pinkertons likely had him in their sights and any one of them probably could have put a bullet in his head any time. Yet Sanderville was a gentleman as well as a hunter. He had honor and would never find satisfaction in letting one of his men shoot a bounty in the back. More importantly, he would never let shooting start with innocent people standing around who might get injured, even if his detectives had the advantage of surprise on their side.

Jason could remember many times when a shooting had

erupted in bloody chaos despite a careful ambush or the best-laid plans. A reflection in an old man's spectacles, a gasp from a bystander, a sound from a shooter's boot as he pivoted to track his target. All of these things had saved Jason's life in the past.

Sanderville was smart and experienced and professional enough to know that the only way to avoid messy situations was to keep control of all variables. Jason knew he would stay alive only as long as he conformed to Sanderville's rules.

He draped his reins loosely over the rail, then stepped back from his horse and pulled his right gun from its holster to check its chamber. The Smith & Wesson Schofield .45-caliber pistol had been his favorite holster gun for the past couple of years. It weighed only two and a half pounds fully loaded, and it was an extremely accurate weapon with its seven-and-a-half-inch barrel.

Designed and invented by an army officer with many years of field experience, the gun was tough and durable, ideal for frontier use. It snapped open easily, as the entire barrel and chamber assembly pivoted forward for quick and easy loading. He found he could save almost two full seconds of loading time over other guns in which the chamber opened and loaded from the side.

With practiced hands, Jason snapped forward the assembly on its pivot and peered into the back end of the chamber. Full with six shells, just as he'd expected.

He closed the chamber and double-twirled the gun back to his holster, mostly just for show. He wanted to unnerve the men he knew were watching him, beginning the essential psychological battle, the war of nerves and mental stamina.

He inspected his left gun the same way, and then pulled both of his belt guns to check them also.

Jason used Colt Peacemakers as his secondary guns. He found the .45-caliber pistol with the short five-and-a-half-inch barrel perfect for a backup belt gun. He always considered the Peacemaker more streamlined than the Schofield. It seemed prettier to him, but in a manly sort of way. He also found them more comfortable to use on account of their one-piece walnut grip. He inspected each gun, careful to make sure the hammer rested on an empty chamber, then stuck the weapons back in his belt.

Jason continued the mental battle and took his time in his preparations. No doubt, the men watching and waiting knew of his reputation with the gun. They were likely anxious already, and he hoped to get them more so. Their nerves would be twanging like a banjo right about now. He hoped to stretch those nerves to the breaking point, see who would make a mistake first.

He reached into a thick pocket on his saddlebag and withdrew a handful of grain. He let his horse eat some from his hand as he talked gently in the animal's ear, then dropped the rest to the ground for the horse to pick at. He took one more look around before he stepped up on the boardwalk in front of the saloon.

Jason had no illusions about how events with the Pinkertons would end. A gunfight against several professional gunmen was fairly hopeless, but he could see no alternatives. Yet as long as he still breathed, he supposed there was at least a hint of a chance.

With his nerves calmed, Jason felt at peace with the inevitability of his situation. He glanced over at Renée-Simone and smiled. She smiled back, and he felt oddly comforted by her gentle eyes. Her companion tugged on her arm, finally coaxing her through the doorway to safety. Jason looked at the wooden slat door of the saloon, then took a deep breath and slowly let it out. Ready as he would ever be, he pushed the door open and walked in.

A dozen men sat at tables in the room, but Jason immediately concentrated his attention on a tall man standing at the bar that stretched along the left wall. Several other men stood along the bar, but Jason knew intuitively they were uninvolved with the Pinkerton detective.

Sanderville looked over as Jason entered. With a head nod he motioned Jason over to join him. Jason scanned the room again as he walked over. Then he studied his opponent and found him to be about what he'd expected of a hardened frontier detective.

Sanderville wore a black three-piece suit over an impeccably clean white shirt and black string tie. His gun rested in a black leather holster high on his right hip. Brown, wavy hair and a long droopy mustache and beard made him look seasoned and experienced.

Round spectacles gave the man an intellectual air, and prominent crow's feet framed his dark brown eyes. High cheekbones and shallow cheeks made him look lean, almost gaunt. Leathery skin gave him the no-nonsense look of a leader.

Jason stopped at the bar, just out of arm's reach. He faced Sanderville and rested his left elbow on the countertop. His right hand hovered near his right holster.

"I hear you're looking for me."

"I am." Sanderville nodded. "Join me for a drink?"

Jason cautiously glanced at the two glasses on the bar in front of Sanderville, then nodded.

"I've never actually been asked to share a drink with a man I'm fixin' to kill."

Jason gazed at the Pinkerton man through emotionless eyes. While his display of gun preparation outside was meant as a psychological challenge to engage an unknown team of men who meant to kill him, the current battle was focused and personal— meant only for the man standing in front of him.

Sanderville just smiled and picked up the closer of two glasses containing a small amount of golden-brown liquid. He held the glass in front of him, swirled the liquid around in the glass, and stared at Jason. In that long moment of intense eye contact, Jason knew without a doubt that Sanderville's interest in him went beyond the requirements of the Pinkerton Agency.

Jason cocked his head and searched Sanderville's eyes for the truth.

"This isn't a Pinkerton operation, is it?" Jason said matter-of-factly. "This is personal. I've killed someone close to you."

Sanderville nodded. "My sister's husband. A man named Fredericks. He was a Texas lawman."

"I remember him." Jason reflected on the deputy-turned-bounty-hunter. "But I never asked him to come around huntin' me."

"Nevertheless, you killed him."

"I reckon I did."

"Well, then. To Mr. Fredericks."

Sanderville raised his drink. Jason reached for his glass and gently touched his rim to Sanderville's.

"To all the idiots who come looking for trouble," Jason taunted. "And die finding it."

Sanderville's eyes twinkled mischievously, but he didn't respond to the challenge. The mental battle continued as both men downed their drinks in a single gulp.

"You have quite a reputation behind you, Mr. Peares. You are the highest-priced outlaw still alive. People we interviewed back in your hometown of Wayne City, Kentucky, consider you a folk hero. Out west, you're a legend. Defender of the weak, helper of the helpless."

The detective continued his recital. "You are exceptionally skilled with a gun." Sanderville nodded as if in approval. "I've heard you're educated also, versed in several languages, and you are well-heeled in the social graces and manners."

"And," Sanderville added, as if to punctuate Jason's history, "you are the dispatcher of twenty lawmen and bounty hunters, as far as we know. The bounty is $7,000."

Sanderville paused and motioned to the bartender, who walked over and poured more whiskey into their glasses.

"I wonder what the bounty will be when I make it twenty-one."

"Actually, it'll have to be twenty-five for you to live to see a higher bounty."

The man just made his first mistake, Jason thought. He'd just told him how many shooters he'd face. Unfortunately, Jason found no advantage in knowing that bit of information.

"And your point is?" Jason said impatiently.

Sanderville patted the badge pinned to his left breast pocket and launched into his formal rhetoric.

"The Pinkerton National Detective Agency has been retained by the governor of the state of Kansas to facilitate your capture. That bounty, by the way, is in gold." He paused. "Dead or alive."

Sanderville adjusted his spectacles. "I've come to kill you."

"Well," Jason said quietly. He took another slight sip of his whiskey and gazed at the detective over the rim. He managed a half-smile, just a twitch of the left side of his mouth, but the smile never quite reached his eyes. "Good luck with that."

CHAPTER 3

SANDERVILLE REACHED FOR HIS OWN glass and took a sip. "Outside then?"

"No," Jason replied, quickly drawing his right gun. He stuck the barrel in front of Sanderville's nose.

Jason scanned the faces in the room. Most of the men just now saw the conflict brewing. Men at the bar behind him suddenly started scrambling to the other side of the room. One man sat in the far corner of the room drinking by himself, staring at Jason. Like Sanderville, he wore a suit, but his was blue and was much more expensive and stylish. He wore no gun, so Jason dismissed him from his attention. He was not a Pinkerton detective.

Sanderville spoke quietly. "Outside we'll give you a chance to pull your guns."

"A chance?" Jason's left eye twitched with anger, and his thumb cocked back the hammer. "Five against one isn't a chance. That's murder."

Sanderville nodded in agreement. "You're an outlaw, Mr. Peares," he said, stating the obvious. "Nobody will complain." Jason remained silent. "I'm offering you the chance to meet your death like a man, standing on your feet."

Jason knew if he killed Sanderville in the saloon he didn't have a prayer of a chance of escaping a siege. The Pinkertons would either rush the saloon and gun him down like a dog, or they'd burn him out. He had no better chance surviving a gunfight out in the street either, but the detective offered no other options.

Jason hated Sanderville and all the lawmen and hunters like him, men who chased Jason for the bounty or for revenge. It was because of men like Sanderville that Jason lived the life of an outlaw. They didn't care that a bigoted sheriff had wrongfully accused him after his first shootout.

He'd found the men who'd killed his family and tried to get a sheriff to arrest them. The sheriff had refused, and the killers had forced him into gunplay. So he'd defended himself. He'd killed four of them and the fifth had run off.

The men who'd hunted him over the years had no intention of giving him a fair trial. Men like Sanderville talked high and mighty about the law or honor, but it was only about the gold. It was simple greed. They kept chasing him, and he kept killing them.

Jason's hand trembled, and he narrowed his eyes. He wanted to kill Sanderville, wanted to make him suffer for all the innocent bystanders who'd been killed when other hunters had found him. With the slightest pressure from his trigger finger, Sanderville would die without a face. Instead, the detective showed no fear. He just stared Jason down, then raised his left hand and moved the gun away from his face.

"I've studied everything about you, Mr. Peares. You're a killer, but not a murderer. Let's take this outside."

Jason slowly put away his gun. As the detective brought up his glass to take another drink, Jason slammed Sanderville's hand against the bar. The whiskey splashed over the countertop and Sanderville's hand.

"Outside then," Jason said.

Sanderville nodded and wiped his wet hand against his vest. Both men turned and walked to the saloon door. At the last moment, Jason stopped at the door and spun around. He found the well-dressed gentleman still staring at him.

"What the hell are you gapin' at?"

The man said nothing and after a moment, Jason turned

toward the door that had already begun to swing closed after Sanderville. He flung the door open hard against the wall. He took a deep breath as he stepped outside, pausing to let his eyes adjust to the blast of sunlight that hurt his eyes after the dimness of the saloon.

He silently cursed himself for losing his temper. He always noted the smallest of details around him, always had an extraordinary sense of his surroundings and what was happening. These professionals had caught him completely unaware, and it unnerved him. It shook his confidence.

In his entire life on the run, seven years now, Jason couldn't remember a time when he'd actually had absolutely no chance, no way out. Today he faced exactly that scenario. He never thought he'd grow old and gray out on the frontier, not as an outlaw. He always figured he'd go down in a blaze of glorious gunfire. Now as he stood outside the saloon and mentally prepared himself for the gunfight, he realized today was that day of glory.

To Jason's right three Pinkerton detectives stood side by side in the middle of the dirt street, facing in his direction. He slowly surveyed the group, recognizing the two who had followed him into town. The one on the right wore a black three-piece suit like Sanderville. The man at the left wore black pants and a black vest over a white shirt. The one in the middle wore typical range clothing.

The vested man held a shotgun, the rancher a Winchester Yellowboy rifle, its brass surfaces cleaned to a shine that reflected the sun with bright sparkles of light when moved just so. The man in the suit wore a single right-handed holster.

The odds were four against one, even though Sanderville had said he'd have to kill five Pinkertons to live through the day. Either the man was playing his own mental game or there was another shooter yet unseen.

No way out.

Jason stepped off the boardwalk, purposely walking behind his horse. To his surprise, Sanderville turned his back to him and walked toward his men. Jason knew this was his chance. The Pinkerton man had made his second mistake.

Jason reached for his gun. Then he heard a metallic click behind him and carefully moved his hand away from his gun. He angled his head to the right and saw the fifth Pinkerton man step from the far side of the saloon, behind him. The man motioned with his gun.

Jason nodded and moved from behind his horse into the middle of the street. The Pinkerton man walked sideways toward his men, covering Jason with his pistol. He stepped between Sanderville and the man in the two-piece suit, then stuck his gun in his holster.

The Pinkertons lined up facing him—vested shotgun, Yellowboy rancher, single gun two-piece suit, single gun fifth man, single gun Sanderville. Those were long odds under any circumstances, and these professionals had a clear strategy Jason had seen played out against other gunfighters and outlaws throughout the frontier.

It wouldn't matter that Jason was no doubt faster than any one of the men facing him. It wouldn't matter that his guns would fire first. Sanderson and his Pinkertons knew their strategy well. Speed of the draw would not be a deciding factor in the outcome of this gun battle. Instead, the outcome would be decided by simple arithmetic. Jason and all the Pinkertons would be pulling iron at the same time. Jason had five targets. The Pinkertons had only one.

He'd panic and rush his shots, trying to hit everyone. He'd miss, trying to adjust his shots in the middle of his draw as he'd realize one or two of the Pinkertons were moving faster than the others. He'd tense his body, knowing hot lead was about to rip into him, and his aim would suffer.

The Pinkertons had safety in numbers, knowing he might get one of them before they got him. They had an 80 percent chance of surviving. He had zero.

Strangely, acceptance of the inevitable outcome that would transpire in a few moments gave Jason a calm serenity, a smoothness of control. He studied the men facing him, looking for any advantage he might use against them.

The vested man on the left was overweight, and as he chewed his tobacco, his double jowls wiggled under his chin. He spat a mouthful of juice that landed with a loud splash in the dirt almost half a dozen paces from his boots. He stood facing slightly away from Jason, with his right hand poised to work the trigger of his shotgun. His left hand gripped the underside of the barrel, holding the weapon against his massive belly with the business end angled down toward the ground.

The man dressed as a ranch hand was tall and stick-thin. He stood ramrod straight and made no movement at all. He held his Yellowboy confidently in his right hand. Poised and ready, he pointed the rifle barrel skyward, finger resting on the trigger. If that man felt any fear at all, Jason could not detect it.

The man in the center fidgeted. He repeatedly flexed his gun hand, trying to disguise his discomfort. Jason knew he had found his first advantage—his own reputation. Sanderville said he had studied everything about Jason. That meant all of the Pinkerton men knew of his skills with guns.

Jason gazed at the nervous man, pressing his advantage. He forced himself not to blink, not to look away. The Pinkerton man flexed his gun hand twice more. Jason kept his gaze locked on the man, but soon the detective couldn't return his stare. The man's right eyelid twitched, and he glanced down at the ground. He bit his lip nervously and flexed his gun hand yet again, this time tightly closing his fist for a whole second.

In his wider field of view, Jason saw the fat man getting ready to spit. At that exact moment, Jason knew he had the best and only opportunity he was ever going to get. A glimmer of hope rushed through him. An impossible situation—his execution—had just become manageable.

Jason knew most people couldn't think fast enough to perform two separate actions at the same time. In fact, he was betting his life that the vested man couldn't spit tobacco and raise his shotgun at the same time. In that brief split second of time, while the first man spat his juice and the third man clenched his fist, Jason faced not five men, but only three.

Arithmetic had given him a chance to survive. Five-to-one odds could not be won, but three to one might possibly be decided by the speed of the draw. He'd beaten those odds before. Maybe he could do it again.

He didn't wait for the Pinkerton men to draw first. As the center man stood frozen, his gun hand clenched, the first man craned his neck to spit. When he jutted his jaw forward and slightly to the side, pursing his lips to let loose the stream of tobacco juice, Jason made his play.

Even as the dark brown fluid left the Pinkerton detective's pursed lips, Jason Peares drew both his holster guns.

CHAPTER 4

OST GUNFIGHTERS MADE AN EXAGGERATED show of putting their whole body into their draw, but Jason considered that a waste of energy and a compromise of speed. Some gunfighters had high-mounted holsters, while others had cross-mounted holsters with the butts facing forward so they could reach across their body. Some turned sideways in the same movement to make a smaller target for their opponent. Some drew with one hand while cocking the pistol by slapping the palm of their other hand down against the hammer. They were all quick or true, but rarely both.

Just before Jason pulled his guns, he faced the Pinkerton detectives calmly with his hands at his sides. He wore a specially designed gun belt with low-slung holster pockets adjusted so his gun butts sat just above the tips of his fingers. All he had to do was just curl his fingers inward, and he had contact with the handles of his Schofield .45s. No wasted arm movement, no exaggerated twisting or jerking his wrists, no spoiling his aim by pounding the gun hammer with the opposite hand.

As he pulled his guns, his index fingers brushed upward along the outside of the holster and curled right into the trigger guards. His thumbs touched lightly against the tops of the cartridge chambers and moved easily back toward the hammers as his guns cleared leather. When the Pinkerton men finally saw Jason's arms moving, they raced to grab or aim their weapons.

With a calmness born of many such contests, Jason gently

thumbed the hammers back. An instant later, he had his guns cocked and perfectly aimed in the time Sanderville and the man next to him took just to clear leather.

He fired both guns at the same time. Sanderville and the man next to him took his first two bullets in their chests. The vested Pinkerton panicked and cut off his spit, though his stream of juice had not hit the dirt yet. He started to raise his shotgun. The man next to him grabbed the underside of the barrel of his Winchester and began to lower the Yellowboy to aim.

Jason staggered his next shots, using the recoil of each shot as momentum to help his thumbs ready his guns. The Winchester man got his third shot, and the shotgun man got his fourth. The unnerved Pinkerton in the middle finally reacted and got his weapon free, and he and Jason fired at the same time.

Jason felt the man's bullet rip through the leather of his left holster as he watched the man's head jerk back in a splatter of blood. Sanderville began to stagger backward a step, still trying to get his gun up.

The man next to Sanderville stumbled back a step, a hand raised to his chest wound. He fell sideways, his mouth wide open in a silent scream and his face a mask of pain. The center man without a face collapsed on top of the fallen man.

The rifle and shotgun men recovered quickly, only wounded from Jason's hastily aimed shots. Jason fired four more times at the two men—left gun, right gun, left gun, right gun. Two shots to the chest of the shotgun, one to the chest and one between the eyes of the Winchester.

Jason fired one last shot at Sanderville and hit him in the chest as the man began to aim again. Then he lowered his guns slowly to his side, his task of survival complete.

The Winchester man died before he fell backward to the ground. The shotgun man took all of Jason's shots in his massive chest without moving. He stood for a while longer, then dropped his weapon and just sat down in the street. Tobacco juice dribbled from his mouth as he leaned his head forward and died sitting there.

Jason quickly scanned the street all around him but saw no other danger. He holstered his guns and walked toward the staggering Sanderville.

Mortally wounded but proud, Sanderville tried to stay on his feet. He swept his arms out wildly to keep his balance as his legs wobbled. Jason quickly stepped close to the man and grabbed him under the arms. Sanderville dropped his gun and fell forward, his hands clutching at Jason's shoulders, eyes drilling into Jason's.

Jason lowered the Pinkerton man slowly to his knees, then held him upright, resting his rump on his boots. Sanderville gasped and tried to talk as blood dribbled from his mouth.

"Nobody...hurt?" he whispered.

Jason looked around. "No innocents took any of our bullets."

"Good." He coughed painfully.

Jason sat silent as the Pinkerton detective tried to speak.

"There'll be more coming after you," he said.

"I know," Jason said. "There always are."

Sanderville's breath rasped loudly, but Jason made no move to leave. Despite his initial anger at the man, he felt a measure of respect and didn't want the man to die alone. He heard boot heels on the boardwalk to his right and realized he might have no choice in the matter.

He looked up to see the kid gunfighter stomping toward him, his nostrils flared and his eyes wide with excitement.

CHAPTER 5

J ASON TURNED EVER SO SLIGHTLY in case he needed to grab one of the guns stuck in his belt. The kid glanced down at Jason's guns and froze. By the time he got his nerve up again, an elderly man stepped from between the buildings near him and pulled him backward by his collar.

Controlled boot steps echoed from the boardwalk behind Jason, and another sound instantly primed him for action. He heard the familiar rustling of air around fabric—a coat or jacket being swept aside to free a gun. He waited for the sound of metal sliding on leather behind him. If he heard it, the shooter would die.

Renée-Simone and her companion stepped onto the boardwalk. Jason caught her gaze for a moment, but she looked away and behind him. He turned his head to see what she saw. The man in the expensive suit stood on the boardwalk in front of the saloon, glaring at him with his hands on his hips. His open jacket revealed a holster mounted under his left armpit.

"You gonna pull that gun, mister?"

Jason looked at the man a moment, glancing at his shoulder holster. He twitched his eyebrow up a bit, inviting him to make his play. The man did nothing, just stood there.

As Jason turned back to face Sanderville, he quickly scanned around him again. Up and down the street, the townsfolk came out of hiding after the conclusion of the spectacle. He saw no immediate danger and finally centered his attention back to

Sanderville. The Pinkerton man trembled uncontrollably. Jason patted his back in a vain attempt to comfort him.

In the beginning, killing the hunters rarely affected him at all. He even enjoyed the excitement and the thrill he always felt as he bested other gunfighters or quick-draw lawmen. Then, one man he'd shot took three hours to die. On an open trail at the mouth of an abandoned mine with no one else around for miles, the young man had begged Jason not to leave him to die alone.

His bullets had chewed up the inside of the man's chest. He held the young man for three of the longest hours of his life, as the man screamed and writhed in pain and agony and slowly bled to death. Since that day, winning the gunfight no longer held any excitement for Jason.

Sanderville coughed and nearly fell over, but Jason steadied him with both hands on his shoulders. The Pinkerton man gasped two more breaths, exhaled finally, and breathed no more. His hands fell away from Jason's shoulders.

Jason laid Sanderville on his side. He retrieved the dead man's hat and covered his face with it. Then Jason stood and adjusted his own hat. He looked around again, wondering if the chase and the killing would ever end. He realized it would end, of course—when he died.

Townsfolk stared at him, but he ignored them and stepped over to the hitching rail in front of the saloon. The man in the expensive blue suit stood on the boardwalk in front of Jason's horse, staring at him.

"Can I help you with something, mister?"

The man stood silently, looking downright sinister. Tall and thin, he stood about Jason's height, a shade over six feet, and had neatly trimmed black hair and mustache. His attitude seemed cocky, arrogant. Jason felt uncomfortable in his presence. He seemed much taller, and his dark, emotionless eyes were unreadable.

"Stay away from my woman," the man said before simply turning away.

Something about him rankled Jason. After pondering a

moment longer, he realized it was probably the snobbish way the man looked down his prominent too-large nose at him. Jason glared at the man's back a while longer, watching his confident stride as he moved away up the boardwalk. Then he dismissed the man from his thoughts and grabbed the reins of his horse. He'd had enough trouble for one day.

Jason cast one last glance at the retreating man and mounted up. He rode his animal in the opposite direction, toward the west end of town. Suddenly, he reined up. He'd bet a month's wages more detectives waited for him out beyond town. He knew instinctively they wouldn't watch the trail he followed into town from the east. That task would be up to the detectives he'd already encountered, but Jason figured any other Pinkerton agents wouldn't know the men in town had changed the plan and tried to satisfy a personal vendetta. A part of him wondered how Sanderville had convinced his men to back him in his personal quest. Maybe Jason had killed some of their kin as well.

He swung his horse around and trotted back up the street toward the east end of town. He passed the saloon where the kid struggled to escape the grip of the man who had grabbed him. The kid said something, and the man whacked him twice upside the head with his hat. Jason passed without stopping, but he heard the final outburst from the kid.

"But, Pa, I can take him!"

Stares followed him as he passed. The slender Frenchwoman, Renée-Simone, and her busty companion stopped walking back to the hotel. They both turned to watch him as he approached. Renée-Simone started to step off the boardwalk, but her companion grabbed her again. The slender woman snatched her arm away, then raised the hem of her dress as she hurried out to meet him.

Jason didn't stop as she approached the middle of the street. He just watched her as she glanced over her shoulder. The man in the expensive blue suit walked up to her companion and spoke harshly. Renée-Simone looked up at Jason.

"May I have a moment, please?" she said in her heavily accented voice. She walked quickly alongside to keep up with him. "I need your help."

"I'm sorry, ma'am. I'm in no position to help you." He looked over at the man standing with Renée-Simone's companion. "I've got enough trouble of my own right now."

"Take me with you then."

"Sorry."

Jason saw the plea in her eyes, almost sensed her need and her desperation. It involved that well-dressed gentleman, he had no doubt. He eyed Renée-Simone's companion with the low-cut dress and dark, fiery eyes. She was definitely trouble of a different kind.

Over the years of outlaw living, Jason had personified trouble as his constant riding partner, always making life difficult for him. He drifted continuously and usually managed to stay invisible, working one cattle run after another, only to wander accidentally into this tiny speck of a town that wasn't even a dot on anybody's map. There he'd found the Pinkerton National Detective Agency waiting to kill him.

Jason spurred his horse into a trot and rode away from the Frenchwoman. Seeing her up close a second time had made him wish he could savor her beauty longer. She was petite, yet very feminine. Her high-necked dress fit the outline of her slender body perfectly.

The smooth, unblemished skin of her face sweetened her smile, though she wore a bit too much color for his liking. Her light brown eyes beckoned him, and her full lips were seductive. Her voice called to him. It reached out and grabbed him. Her French accent was music to his ears, intimate and personal.

Jason fought the urge to look back and see if Renée-Simone still stood in the street. Whatever she wanted, he would never know. He had to put as much distance between himself and Franklin Town as possible before the Pinkertons struck up his trail again.

He knew they would. They had a reputation to protect. They never quit.

CHAPTER 6

THE FIRST WEEK HE PUSHED hard and followed well-traveled trails. The Pinkerton trackers would have a difficult time separating his tracks from hundreds of others. They'd pick up his trail eventually, though. Of this he was more than certain. So he rode for three weeks, doubling back several times and tracing circles around his imaginary pursuers.

He rode deep into the hills south of Franklin Town, always backtracking. Finally, he found a primary road leading back toward the town from the southwest. Three miles shy of town he struck out due west to make his pursuers think he was finally attempting to escape the county. Then just five days later, he came across a stream twelve miles farther west. He guessed a larger river fed the stream but had no idea if the source was ten miles north or a hundred.

Jason guided his horse into the water and headed upstream to the northwest. The Pinkerton detectives would track him to the stream, then try to guess which way he went. To be thorough, they'd have to split up to track upstream and downstream and cover both banks for his exit. They'd find no sign of him until he wanted them to, and they'd use up a lot of supplies in the process. It was all part of the ongoing mental battle. Right when they'd think they'd found his trail, they'd have to regroup and resupply, losing time.

Pinkerton Detective Agency hired the toughest frontier men with unmatched hunting skills, but they were civilized lawmen.

They had wives and children back home somewhere. They didn't live off the land for months, or even years, like Jason. They didn't sleep on the hard ground in all kinds of weather. While they excelled at hunting men, they usually weren't as adept at hunting varmints to eat.

Foraging for edible fruits, nuts, and critters was as much a part of Jason's daily life as breathing, and he never rode the trail without an emergency supply of hardtack and beans that could last him weeks with careful rationing.

He thought back on all the pursuits he had survived over the years. He'd eluded dozens of such pursuers, including some of the most dedicated posses ever assembled. Some chases lasted only a few days or weeks, others dragged on for months. A few ended in ambush, usually with Jason doing the ambushing. Still fewer ended in an actual gunfight in the middle of a frontier town or a forest outpost or a mining colony.

The famous Marshal Gallagher had chased him for more than two years. That pursuit, like most, ended with no resolution, as his pursuers either lost his trail or lost their motivation and quit.

Each chase brought Jason more wisdom and more survival skills. He always matched his pursuers' professionalism and determination. He always managed to outwit the trackers. As the years passed, life on the run became as comfortable as eating or drinking. It was not something to regret or hope to change. It did not wear him down. It simply was a way of life.

Jason kept his horse in the water four full days. He never ventured onto dry land or left any sign. He napped briefly each night with the reins wrapped around his wrist while squatting on a boulder when he could find one in the middle of the stream. Some nights he simply sat in the shallow, warm water.

He thought about the Frenchwoman and wondered what circumstances had brought such a woman to a dusty town in the middle of Kansas. He wondered what kind of trouble she was in that enabled her to ask a known outlaw and killer to take her with him. He tried to push from his mind the memory of his brief encounter with her and concentrate on his current situation. He had to make his move soon or he'd be in the same situation he hoped to put his hunters in—out of supplies.

His biggest concern was the health of his horse. He cared for the animal as best he could. He checked its hooves every now and again and rested the animal frequently. He hand-fed it small rations of grain because it couldn't graze without leaving indications of his passage. Until he was ready, he couldn't leave any sign the Pinkertons would pick up.

He pecked at his diminishing supply of dried beef jerky every morning, noon, and night. On the morning of the fourth day, he rewarded the Pinkerton trackers for their diligence.

The stream narrowed to only a few feet as it tumbled over a small field of rocks that appeared suddenly in the otherwise flat landscape. He dismounted and led his horse up the gentle rise in the stream. He let the horse feed on tufts of grass growing in the shallow water between the rocks and along the bank. Just a little bit here and there, so only the keenest eye would spot any sign of torn grass.

He expected his followers would rejoice in discovering his trail after four grueling days of pursuit. They'd be cautious, even suspicious, of a deception. Five hours later, they'd find more cleverly concealed rips of grass upstream that Jason's feeding horse made. Then the trackers would know there was no deception. They would think they had won the battle of patience and caution.

Jason knew professionals such as the Pinkertons approached the task of tracking their prey very seriously. They would never indulge in wild and emotional chases, finally catching their quarry on slathering and spent horses. There would be no fiery gun battles to punctuate the capture. Professional trackers used patience and preparation as their primary weapons. They conserved their supplies and horses because they never knew how long the chase would take. When they crossed the sign of their target, the professionals would regroup to readjust their strategy and to resupply if necessary.

The Pinkerton trackers would proceed carefully with a plan calculated to wear him down emotionally, mentally, and physically. They would pursue him relentlessly, anticipating and cutting off all avenues of potential escape. They'd patiently surround him in an invisible noose, and then move in with a carefully orchestrated attack, almost military in its precision, until either he surrendered or they killed him. Jason had seen such professional tactics before and when they tried to close the trap this time, he would be miles away.

He figured only two, maybe three trackers followed him upstream. When they crossed his sign, one or two of the men would stay behind and make camp, waiting for one rider to collect the southbound trackers. They'd probably resupply and get fresh mounts before heading back north. Tracking was slow business, but Jason figured the Pinkertons could be ready to get back on his trail in less than two days.

Just as the professional Pinkerton hunters took a calculated approach to pursuing their prey, Jason was just as cunning at evasion. He'd had many years of practice. Hastily organized posses were the easiest to evade as they rarely had enough preparation or stamina for more than a couple days of pursuit. Professional hunters, on the other hand, required that he match wits with them.

There was no anger or frustration or wishful thinking involved in Jason's plans. Evasion and survival were what he was good at. It was easy for him. So it was completely natural for him to consider what his pursuers would do and how they would react. That way he could always stay ahead of them.

It was critical for Jason to travel slow enough not to get too far ahead of his pursuers. Figuring they were no more than a day behind him, he backtracked in the stream, knowing with a fair amount of confidence that they were camped in the stand of trees he'd seen by the narrow part of the stream. That was where he would camp if he were tracking someone.

He passed the camp two hours before dawn. If anyone was awake, he knew their attention would be at its lowest. As he figured, the camp was tucked way back in the trees, almost a hundred paces off the bank of the stream. He smelled the faint wisp of smoke, carried on the slight morning breeze, from the campfire they'd allowed to burn down from a late dinner. They were safe from ambush but too far away to see his passing in the dark of the early hour.

Jason whispered to his horse to keep the animal quiet as he led the animal past the trees. He was certain the trickle of the water over the rocks would cover any noise his horse might make. Still, he led the animal slowly and carefully.

For the briefest instant of time, he considered sneaking into the camp and eliminating the men, but that thought passed quickly. It disturbed him that Sanderville had known him so deeply, but it was certainly a fact that he was not a murderer. He couldn't justify taking two or three lives just for a minor tactical advantage. Besides, his strategy was to lead the hunters astray, not to leave bodies that would reveal his location.

Jason had covered his pack with his rain slicker so no metal buckles would reflect light from the quarter moon sitting low in the western sky. He wore his winter long coat for the same reason, to blend better with the darkness. The midsummer night temperature was almost as hot as daytime and after a couple of hours his shirt was drenched with sweat under the heavy coat.

Four hours later, Jason stopped to bathe and wash his sweat-soaked shirt in the stream. Afterward, he left the stream by its east bank and headed southeast back toward Franklin Town, knowing his successful escape was due as much to luck as skill.

When he left the stream, he crossed the tracks made by a slow careful rider heading north, likely a tracker searching earlier for Jason's sign. Then he saw the tracks of a horse at a trot, likely the man going back for the other Pinkertons. He hoped the returning posse would be riding fast, retracing the path of the rider sent to fetch them. He hoped they wouldn't be looking for Jason's tracks since his sign had already been cut farther north.

At best, he'd lose them completely and eventually continue

his journey back down to Texas to put in for more ranch work. At worst, they'd continue north for a while until they figured out that he'd outsmarted them and doubled back yet again. In that case he might gain another two days on them. If they picked up his trail again, they'd be fairly discouraged to find that he had led them in a big circle back to their starting place.

The mental battle continued.

Jason rode southeast for a long while, then followed a trail south. Just after nightfall, he realized the trail did not lead back to Franklin Town as he expected but swung due east to another sprawling town. He paused beside a sign stuck in the dirt beside the trail and looked in his packs for a match. After searching through several pockets, he finally found one and struck it against his saddle horn.

The sign read Salina.

As always, the darkness of the night became his friend, and he rode in on one of the side streets. He wove his horse through the disorganized gaggle of paths between the collection of shacks and cabins, heading vaguely toward the lamps at the center of town.

Occasionally, a dog barked or trotted alongside his horse. Every now and then a face appeared in a darkened window or a shadow studied him from a doorway. No lamps lit the next side street he turned onto, but presently he found a stable open on the south side of town, despite the late hour. A dark-haired boy about fourteen or so sat on a stool outside the stable door whittling a stick. A coin to the lad got Jason a promise of excellent care and feed for his horse.

Before he left the stable, he packed away his holster and guns, instead leaving a single short-barrel Colt Peacemaker tucked into the front of his belt. He didn't know if any lawmen or Pinkerton detectives might be in town looking for him, though he guessed word of his gunfight in Franklin Town had already reached Salina. They'd be looking for a man wearing a double-gun rig. Besides, with several week's razor stubble, Jason knew he didn't resemble his Wanted poster very closely.

He made his way up another side street and cut between some shacks. He emerged onto the main street just beside the saloon and glanced up and down the street. Several lamps burned in front of the two hotels and the saloon. Jason studied the people crossing the street or walking along the boardwalk in the lamplight. *Just ordinary folk,* he concluded. They were no danger to him.

The flame from a gas lamp flickered brightly over the boardwalk outside the double swinging doors of the saloon. His gut told him to avoid the noisy place and its crowd, but his parched throat demanded attention. Besides, he needed information about where he could find a room and a bath at this late hour. Maybe he could discretely find out if anyone in town might be looking for him.

With his hat stuck low over his eyes, Jason pushed his way through the double doors.

CHAPTER 7

IMMEDIATELY, THE HARSH SIGHTS AND sounds of frontier night life assaulted his senses. The saloon was larger than most he'd seen. A couple dozen crowded tables were scattered haphazardly around the room. Catcalling men watched a trio of scantily clad saloon girls dancing on the elevated stage midway along the right wall. The girls tried to keep up some semblance of coordinated movements as the raucous audience threw coins at them.

Bodies packed the busy room. There were smelly cowboys and ranch hands, well-dressed cigar-smoking businessmen, and perfumed ladies of the night. Jason shoved his way to the bar along the left wall. An overly large woman with a fake smile on her face turned suddenly away from the bar. The sight of her conjured up the words of an old miner Jason had come across in years past.

I like my frontier women painted and hard-boiled.

Jason narrowly dodged his head away from her elevated tray of drinks as she left the bar. He quickly stepped into the space left by her departure, then signaled the barkeep and waited for the man to come and get his order. Absently, he watched the woman with her tray of drinks make her way toward a table across the room, sometimes shoving men out of her way.

She set her tray on top of the card game of some nearly drunk men, but they seemed not to notice. With one hand, the woman distributed the drinks. With her other hand, she brushed away hands groping at her plump body. Then she plopped herself down in the lap of one of the more intoxicated men and pretended to enjoy his company.

She worked the man quickly and professionally. She grabbed some coins from his hand, then rose and literally dragged him by a suspender strap toward a hallway leading to the back of the saloon.

Jason traded a coin for a tall glass of lightly colored liquid and took a long, satisfying drink, draining half the glass. He wiped froth from his upper lip with the back of his shirtsleeve, took a deep breath, and drained the rest of the glass. He savored the bitter taste of the beer, felt its wetness soothe his dry throat, then held up his glass for a refill.

The entire room erupted in wild cheers and shouts for more as the dancers finished their performance. The three dancers gathered up all the coins, then stepped down from the stage and made their way toward the tables of rich businessmen.

Several men in the crowd rose from their tables to leave after the performance. Three men, all dressed in black three-piece suits, had risen from a table he hadn't seen behind a group of standing men. Jason froze. They turned and walked toward him.

Frontier cowboy detectives! They had to be. They wore guns and tin badges, and they even moved with the swagger of Pinkerton men!

He had only seconds before they spotted him, but he had nowhere to go. Hemmed in by the crowd of men swarming to the bar after the performance, he was pressed against the bar by bodies on both sides. By the time he could extricate himself from the bar, the lawmen would be right in front of him. In desperation, he reached for the gun at his belt.

Before he could pull it free, a small but strong hand gripped his gun hand and kept the weapon in place.

"There you are, darling!"

A woman had forced her way through the crowd of three-deep men the way only a woman could. She grabbed him by the shoulders and spun him sideways a bit, then grabbed his face and pulled him forward. She kissed him and pivoted toward the bar, turning him with her.

He recognized her. The curly black hair, round face full of color and smiles, the enormous bosom barely restrained by the tight fabric of her dress. She was Bonnie Drake—the curvy companion of the Frenchwoman from Franklin Town.

He watched her eyes as she watched the detectives moving behind him. When she relaxed and wrapped her arms around his neck, he sensed he was out of danger and let himself be caught up in a fiery kiss.

She was gutsy and strong, a hardened frontier woman, and her fast thinking had just saved his life. *She's also an excellent kisser,* he thought as her tongue expertly wrestled with his for a few moments. Finally, she pulled away and took a deep breath.

"Well, that was nice," she said, smiling.

"And timely. I'm obliged to you, Miss Drake."

"I'm flattered you remember my name."

Jason scanned the room again, more carefully this time, but he saw no other detectives or lawmen. He felt very foolish for taking the risk of stopping in town and walking into a crowded saloon. He took a deep breath, realizing how close he had come to a disastrous gunfight.

Jason looked at the woman clinging to him. Her body pressed against his, her flesh inviting. She smiled seductively, and he inhaled the heady scent of her perfume and tasted the faint flavor of whiskey on her breath. Her face was a mask of color around her eyes, cheeks, and lips. Heavy powder attempted to conceal deep lines at the corners of her eyes. He could see the years had not been kind to her. She was not unattractive, but that old miner would have had words to describe this particular working saloon girl.

Powder and paint make a woman what she ain't.

Jason moved his hands from her waist to her arms. She took the hint and unwrapped her arms from his neck. Self-consciously, she tucked a loose tangle of hair behind her ear as he studied her.

"She kept saying you would come back to rescue her, but I just told her she was dreaming."

"What? Who?"

"Renée-Simone," Bonnie said. "The French girl you saw with me in Franklin Town."

Bonnie nodded over his shoulder, and he followed her gaze toward the ornate spiral staircase beyond the stage. Renée-Simone stood at the top of the stairs, leaning on the balcony rail. She wore an expensive cream-colored gown, formfitting and V-cut down the front. Glittering jewels adorned her neck. She turned her back on a man who shouted in her ear.

"She sure had me fooled," Jason said.

He'd thought about the Frenchwoman several times over the weeks on the trail, knowing full well he'd never see her again. She'd lived in his memory as he'd last seen her, beautiful and vulnerable. In his imagination, she was something other than what she really was.

"I never figured her for a working girl."

"She ain't." Bonnie looked at Jason briefly, then glanced away with sadness in her eyes. "Well, not yet, not really. It's her first night on the job. She's not really made out for this kind of work. I've been trying to keep her out of the saloon, but she's... got some problems."

He looked up again, saw Renée-Simone wince as a man standing behind her shouted at her again. Jason recognized the businessman from Franklin Town. The man wore a light gray suit with a high-collared white shirt. A black top hat completed his suit. He held a gentleman's cane in his right hand.

"Who's the obnoxious fellow?" Jason said.

"Albert Danton. He's her...manager. Not the kind of man you say no to."

Jason saw Renée-Simone and Danton exchange harsh words, and Danton grabbed her arm as she tried to walk away from him. She twisted free, fumbling a small beige handbag she carried in her left hand. She recovered and ran down the curved stairs, cradling her left forearm. She made her way through the crowd, toward the front door.

Jason watched her move through the crowd that seemed to magically part before her. She looked sophisticated and elegant. She looked expensive. The crowd of men closed in behind her, gaping at her as she passed. None moved to pursue her. Jason knew they could never afford such a woman in a dozen lifetimes.

Bonnie started to call out to Renée-Simone, but Jason stopped her.

"I didn't come here to get involved in her troubles."

"But I saw you face Danton in Franklin Town. You're not afraid of him. You could take her away from here, keep her safe. She'll go with you. I know she will."

Jason shook his head. "As you've noticed, I've got plenty of troubles of my own."

He looked around as if expecting the Pinkerton detectives to walk back into the saloon.

"Don't worry about them. I overheard one earlier say they had to ride out with some supplies for one of their posses."

"At night?"

She shrugged. "If you ask me, I think they're supposed to be out there right now with the rest of their men, hunting for you." She playfully poked him in the chest. "Probably should've been on the trail instead of in here drinking. And they're none too happy about it either.

"Anyway," she added with a teasing smile. Her sadness over Renée-Simone's plight vanished and she was back to business. "I know somewhere safe you can spend the night where no one will find you."

Before he could respond, Bonnie wrapped her arms around his neck and kissed him again. She pressed against him as he meekly tried to get free.

"That damned gun is in the way," she said, grinding her hips against his. "That is your gun, isn't it?" She looked down and snickered.

"It's a nice thought, but I don't want what you're sellin'."

He knew she was working him just as professionally as the other saloon girl had gotten her client. He put a little space between them and changed the subject.

"Maybe you could tell me where I can get some dinner and a bath. Then, I'm ridin' out. Can't hang around here with the Pinkertons so close."

"Give me two dollars, and I'll cook you dinner myself." She teased him with another lingering look that drifted downward and back up again. "And breakfast."

"I'm grateful for your help, but I can't bed a woman who does what you do."

"You don't say! How long has it been, Cowboy?"

She looked at him as if she could see the answer in his eyes. It had been a while. It had been a long while.

"Thought so. I just give comfort for lonely drifters like yourself, that's all. How long will it be before you settle in somewhere, maybe find yourself a nice young lady? A month? A year?" She nestled back close to him. "Come on, I know you got two dollars in your pocket, don't you?"

"No, thanks."

"You sure? I'll give you a night to remember. Ever been with a real experienced lady like me?"

"Never have, never will. My ma taught me better."

"That's what mothers are supposed to do. But I'm sure if we ask her, she'll admit to understanding that grown men have needs."

"My ma's dead, so she won't be answering any questions."

His mother and the rest of his family had been murdered. He flashed back to a distant memory when he had hunted down the murderers and killed them in return. Bonnie Drake seemed to sense the quick change in Jason's demeanor.

"I'm sorry," she said gently. "I didn't know."

He nodded. "It was a while ago."

"Listen," Bonnie continued. "Why not try the Hotel Salina up the street? Their kitchen stays open late. I gotta get back to work now. Come get me if you change your mind."

Bonnie touched him on the shoulder, turned, and walked away. She left so suddenly, Jason didn't have time to tell her that her lip color was all smeared from kissing on him. He watched her a moment as she swayed over to a table of men starting a card game. Then he turned back to the bar and took a long drink of his second beer. He wiped his mouth again and noticed the stain of Bonnie's lip color on his sleeve.

Jason savored the flavor of the beer, the fragrance of Bonnie Drake, the memory of her closeness. Two dollars. That's all that separated him from a night of companionship. He closed his eyes a moment, tasting her kiss again in his memory.

He'd been in town too long already. The Pinkerton detectives could return at any moment. Bonnie could hide him all night. Even as he turned to look for her in the crowd, Jason argued all the reasons why he shouldn't find her.

Forget about companionship and hot grub. He had to get out of town fast. Bonnie Drake wouldn't be around to save him if he got careless a second time. He finally saw her at the card players' table, working the half-drunk men. In his side vision, he noticed movement at the top of the stairs.

Danton conversed with an elderly man with white hair and a huge belly. He wore brown pants and a tan shirt with a silver string tie. Money changed hands and the old man hobbled down the stairs, his attention set singularly on the saloon doors.

Jason knew the Frenchwoman had her first customer. He turned back to the bar, feeling a twinge of confusion. Seeing how she had refused the obnoxious man, Jason couldn't help but wonder if this was the trouble she was in. Had she been somehow conscripted into working the saloon crowd and had reached out to him to take her away?

Taking a deep breath, Jason tried to dismiss Bonnie Drake and the Frenchwoman from his mind. What she was going through was none of his business, and he certainly didn't have the wherewithal to rescue her.

He downed the rest of his beer and turned away from the bar. He took one last glance up at the balcony and was not at all surprised to see Albert Danton staring right at him. In Franklin Town, the man had struck Jason as an observer of details, so it was just a matter of time before the man found him in the crowd. He held Danton's stare. After a few seconds, he realized Danton wasn't going to be the first to break the eye contact, so Jason turned away and started for the door.

He paused just before pushing through the doors because an uncomfortable feeling had clenched his gut, and he knew he had to confirm it. He turned and saw Danton moving down the last steps of the stairs. He walked straight toward Jason. Their gazes locked, and Jason could only think of one word.

Trouble.

CHAPTER 8

J ASON PASSED THROUGH THE DOUBLE swinging doors. Danton was coming after him, and it had something to do with the Frenchwoman. He felt no fear, but he certainly knew he had to get out of town immediately to avoid the confrontation and the attention it would focus on him. People would see him and remember him. They'd tell the Pinkerton detectives about him. The hot meal and bath would have to wait. He never should have ridden into town at all.

A scuffle caught his attention directly to the right of the doors. Renée-Simone struggled to elude the grasp of her client as the man clumsily tried to kiss her. She twisted away from the man's grip and stumbled right into Jason's arms.

He held her for the briefest of moments as he kept her from falling. Slowly, gently, he lifted her upright.

She gasped. "You came back!"

"Hey!" Her client stomped forward. "She's mine! I paid good money for her."

With Renée-Simone still in his grasp, Jason sidestepped as the man reached out clumsily to grab her. Then he grabbed the man's wrist and twisted, pulling him forward and off-balance. He yanked down hard, bending him over at the waist. He spun him toward the saloon door, stuck a boot against his rump, and shoved. The man stumbled back through the saloon doors with his arms flailing.

Jason turned back to Renée-Simone and stared at her for

a few seconds that seemed like an eternity. He inhaled her fragrance. Her perfume was different from Bonnie's, more subtle. It was a tantalizing, lingering scent he'd never smelled before. When he'd pushed the drunk man away, she had stepped closer to him, and now her face was only inches from his. Her brown eyes glowed, or was that his imagination? Nothing existed except the exotic scent of the Frenchwoman and the seductive accent of her sultry voice.

Seeing her from across the room held no comparison to standing next to her. She was stunningly beautiful, Jason realized as he studied her long brown hair and her flawless skin and her formfitting silk dress. Renée-Simone blushed and passed a hand through her hair.

"Sorry, ma'am. I didn't mean to stare."

She smiled briefly, nervously, then said, "Can you help me? Can you take me with you? Away from here?" Her eyes searched his, her gaze full of desperation.

"Can't do that, ma'am. I'm ridin' out straightaway."

She started to speak but hesitated, looking over his shoulder. The saloon doors squeaked on their hinges, and Jason smelled bittersweet cigar smoke. He glanced over his shoulder and saw Danton standing just outside the doors. The man nonchalantly puffed on a half-burned stogie, but Jason didn't remember noticing him holding the cigar before. He was distracted by this lovely woman and his lack of attention bothered him.

Renée-Simone whispered, her accented voice soft and sensuous. "Wherever you're going, take me with you. Please."

"Renée!" Danton said. "You have a client inside, pitiful as he may be. But he's already paid."

"I'm going with him," Renée-Simone said defiantly, grabbing Jason's arm with both hands.

"You'll take the clients I tell you to take. Besides," Danton continued, puffing strongly on his cigar with an air of sophistication, "he can't afford you."

"I won't work for you." She looked at Jason quickly and added, "I'm not a whore."

"Not yet." Danton snickered. "But you will be after tonight. And there's nothing this half-breed can do about it."

Jason could have and should have let the challenge pass and just ridden out of town. He would have let it pass, too, except for that word. A year ago, Jason had shot a man in the leg for calling him a half-breed. As far back as he could remember, he'd hated that word and anyone who uttered it.

He removed Renée-Simone's hands from his arm and stepped over to face Danton. Sure, his gut instinct told him to leave the Frenchwoman to her own affairs. This man, Danton, was taunting him, though. Both men knew it, and Jason refused to walk away from the challenge.

Danton stuck the cigar back in his mouth and pulled deeply. He looked Jason straight in the eyes and blew out a long stream of smoke into his face. Jason quickly held his breath, but the smoke burned his eyes. He turned away, blinking rapidly, eyes watering.

Without warning, Jason rammed his left fist forward and caught Danton in the belly. The man dropped to his knees with a loud explosion of air and gasped. Jason balled his eyes with his fists, then wiped tears away with the back of his sleeve. He knelt beside Danton and retrieved the dropped cigar.

Jason rubbed his burning eyes again as he waited for Danton to catch his breath. It was too late to avoid trouble, he realized. His insane need for a drink and a hot meal, which he was going to have to leave town without, had gotten him involved in an altercation. The news that Jason Peares had been in town would spread like a wildfire, and the Pinkertons would be back on his trail within hours.

He glanced over his shoulder at Renée-Simone. He wasn't sure what her story was, but getting involved in the trouble of others was what he did. He helped people who couldn't help themselves, especially when there were men like Danton involved.

When Albert Danton sucked in a deep breath to speak, Jason grabbed him by the hair. He jerked the man's head back and examined the glowing end of the cigar Danton had dropped. He jammed it hard against Danton's left cheek and held it there while the man whimpered and tried vainly to escape. The cigar sizzled as Jason extinguished the embers on Danton's skin.

Danton gasped in pain, then Jason shoved him back against the wall of the saloon. As Danton grabbed his cheek, Jason stood and flipped the dead cigar to the boardwalk beside the man. He stepped over to Renée-Simone.

He couldn't leave her. Not now. She'd defied Danton, stood behind Jason's implied protection. If he turned away now, left her without that protection, she'd suffer Danton's wrath. She'd be a slave, a whore, maybe even get killed. Jason couldn't let that happen.

He considered his options. Eventually, the Pinkertons would pick up his trail to Salina. Now, it was likely someone from Salina, maybe Danton himself, would send word to the detectives that he was here. So he couldn't stay around and deal with Danton or get involved in whatever business the man had going on. Nor could he take Renée-Simone with him. Running from the Pinkertons, he could hardly guarantee her safety. Hell, he couldn't even ensure his own safety.

He offered his left arm to Renée-Simone and began to escort her up the boardwalk. After three steps, he stopped almost in midstride as he heard a familiar sound behind him.

"I know what you're thinking, mister. I'm facing away from you, and you've got a pretty good grip on that piece in your shoulder holster. Maybe you've got it halfway out. Maybe you're even thinkin' you can finish pullin' your gun before I can pull mine. Maybe you're thinking you can shoot me before I can turn and put a bullet in your skull."

Jason paused, listening for the sound of Danton's gun sliding out of his holster. "But if I were you, I'd be thinkin' real hard about what I saw in Franklin Town." Jason paused again, still listening. "Now, why don't you let go of that gun nice and slow, 'cause you're real close to meetin' your maker."

He looked over his shoulder as Danton carefully pulled his

hand from inside his suit jacket. He got to his feet, stared at Jason a moment longer, and went back into the saloon.

"What do we do now?" Renée-Simone said.

"I have no idea," he said, facing her. She managed a nervous smile and blushed again as he stared at her.

No two ways about it, the woman was beautiful. The elegant silk dress accentuated her perfect curves. The fabric glistened in the lamplight as though sprinkled with hundreds of tiny diamonds. She was truly a vision of loveliness.

"I'll have to figure out something real quick, though. I don't want to be around tomorrow when the sheriff makes his rounds. He hears I'm in town, he might try to be a hero, or he might send someone out to round up those Pinkertons."

Jason paused. "We'll be safe from the law tonight. A man like Danton won't call the sheriff. He has other ways to handle problems. He operates outside the law, so right now Danton is much more dangerous than any lawman. We just need somewhere to hide until daybreak. Come on. I've got an idea." They stepped off the boardwalk.

"So," he said, leading Renée-Simone into the darkness. "What's your story with that man?"

CHAPTER 9

JASON LED RENÉE-SIMONE TO THE north side of town, then west and back south to the stable where he'd left his horse. There were only a couple horses in the stable, and the animals shifted a bit as Jason chose a stall near the back. He began pushing a pile of straw into the empty stall for their bed. Then he removed his hat and gun belt.

Renée-Simone stood by the waist-high stall door and said, "We're sleeping in a barn? On the floor?"

"Think of it as a new adventure." He made himself comfortable and patted the straw next to him. "I guarantee you no one will come looking for you here."

She settled in next to him, but he could tell sleeping next to a complete stranger was as uncomfortable for her as it was for him. They lay quietly for a long while, staring into the darkness above them. Eventually, she began talking, but then a brief pause stretched into a long silence, and he realized she'd fallen asleep.

He rolled onto his side and watched her sleep. Her face seemed so peaceful, so innocent and pure. She awoke briefly once and smiled when she noticed him watching her, then she rolled into him and cuddled against his chest. He held her for a while and considered what she'd told him.

Danton was a predator and had ensnared her when she was most vulnerable. Jason had heard the same type of tale countless times over the years. The names and faces were different, as were the circumstances, but the outcome was always the same. The strong triumphed over the weak.

Robbers had attacked her stagecoach and shot Renée-Simone's husband and two other men for no good reason. Danton had miraculously turned up in time to prevent her from suffering a fate much worse than death. He was a caring, concerned gentleman who paid her expenses, buried her husband, and paid off the taxes on her house when she had no means to make the payments. He helped her get back on her feet again.

When she'd decided to move back to New Orleans to rejoin her kinfolk, his demeanor changed. She owed him. He'd threatened her, then beat her, and made it clear that he owned her. He'd told her no one could help her and no one would rescue her. If anyone even tried, he'd have them killed.

If she wanted to live, she would have to live the way he said, doing what he told her to do. He scared her out of her mind. She'd seen the results of his threats on other men and women. Those who tried to run away, he found and punished. Danton controlled Renée-Simone, and she had no defense against him. She had no protection from the terror he caused.

Bonnie Drake had befriended her and helped her survive, but the weeks of threats and intimidation had worn her down. She'd finally broken down to Danton's will. Tonight, her first night at the saloon, she was to get her first customer. Danton had purchased a room in the Hotel Salina for her, next door to Bonnie's room.

Then Jason had showed up. She knew him by reputation and had heard much about him from the Pinkerton detectives in Franklin Town. Even before the gunfight that ended badly for the detectives, she knew Danton would not be able to intimidate him. He was her salvation, or so she thought.

"We went to Franklin Town so Mr. Danton could do some banking business," she'd said earlier. "We'd just arrived when the Pinkerton detectives rode in and warned everyone you might be headed there. I knew you could stand up to him. I prayed that you'd come back. And here you are."

"Right," Jason had answered skeptically. "Put your life in the hands of an outlaw you don't even know, a man who is a wanted killer. I can't say that's the smartest of plans."

He understood her desperation. She would do anything and take any risk to escape Danton.

What seemed like only minutes later, Jason awoke to an awful racket. Then someone opened the stable doors and sunlight spilled in. It took a moment for him to remember where they were.

He recalled two rows of horse stalls in the stable. The first row stretched from the stable doors all the way to the back, ten stalls on the right side, eight on the left. They had settled in the last stall on the right. Half walls separated each of the stalls, keeping their bed of straw in deep shadow. He remembered that when he had ridden to the stable the night before, the stable boy had led his horse down a short corridor to the left of the stable doors and bedded his horse down in one of the stalls in the second row.

Jason settled back down in the straw beside Renée-Simone. She cuddled closer to him, grabbed his hand, and wrapped his arm around her. He tensed. There was something about this woman he felt was not quite right, but he couldn't wrap his mind around the feeling. Her story was reasonable, but his gut told him it seemed contrived. Her vulnerability seemed too convenient. Her appearance and that of the Pinkertons, both in Franklin Town and now again here in Salina, was a bit too coincidental, though he had no rational reason to suspect that.

His straight-thinking mind told him there couldn't possibly be a connection between this woman and the detectives. Yet his gut told him to be suspicious of her wiles. He was certain she was not quite what she appeared to be. She was using him.

He whispered. "How do you feel?"

"Safe."

"We'll have to leave soon."

They lay together for a while, enjoying the comfort of each other's warmth. Realizing they needed to make a move sooner rather than later to avoid detection, Jason stood and stretched. After a moment, Renée-Simone stood, and they brushed straw from their hair and clothes.

"Let's get you on the next stagecoach, no matter where it's going. It'll take you to a train that you can take home to New Orleans. I'll ride with you for a few days just to make sure Danton doesn't send men after you."

She hugged Jason tightly. "I knew you would help me." She kissed him on the cheek. "Can I stop by my house and pack some things?"

He shook his head. "Not a good idea. I know his type. I figure Danton will have men all over town looking for us. Chances are good he's got a man watching your house. We've got to go straight to the stagecoach. If we're lucky, he'll think we rode out last night. You can get on the stage without being seen."

"In the middle of town?" she said. "Mr. Danton practically lives at the Hotel Salina. It's right across the street from the stagecoach office."

"Well," Jason said, "then I invite him to show his face. Let's go."

He led the way through the stable, past the surprised stable boy. Jason bridled and saddled his horse, then tied his packs in place. He paid the stable boy another dollar for his help and for their use of the extra stall. Then he buckled on his two-gun rig and tied the leg straps at the bottom of each holster. Task complete, Jason checked everything again and stuck his belt gun in his saddle pack. He checked both holster guns and found the Schofields, of course, fully loaded.

He helped Renée-Simone settle sideways into the saddle and climbed up behind her. They rode over one street south of the main street and tied up where few people were about. Jason led the way between two stores, into an alley just behind the stagecoach office. Cautiously, he scanned the street again for anyone who looked like they might be looking for them.

"I'm going to see when the next stage leaves and get your ticket," Jason said. He reached into his pocket, handed her some coins. "Buy yourself some comfortable clothes for the trail." He nodded at the back of the general store next door. "Go in that way."

They parted, but Jason stared after her as she walked away. She was beauty in formfitting silk, and he wondered things that men always seemed to think when gazing upon a fine woman. He turned away and shook his head. *No use even thinking those crazy thoughts.*

Unfortunately, holding her while she'd slept had already ignited the fire within him.

Being needed was a good feeling, but she seemed too comfortable with him. It almost felt like she knew him, which, of course, was impossible.

The general store had a back door for Renée-Simone to use, but the stage office didn't, so Jason went around to the front. He paused at the edge of the boardwalk, surprised to see the coach waiting. A man packed baggage up top and four passengers waited to board.

He scanned the main street up and back. Seeing no danger, he walked to the stage office door on his right and took one last glance around before entering. The Hotel Salina stood across the street, two buildings east. He saw no activity there. Several buildings farther to the east, the midday drinkers were starting to file into the saloon.

He bought a ticket east to Kansas City and asked the driver to wait five minutes before making his last call. Shouting thanks, he ran out the door and into the general store to get Renée-Simone. He grabbed the first pants and shirt he saw, threw them at her, and paid while she changed. Suspenders held up her too-large pants. Scuffed boots and a second-hand hat finished out her outfit.

She grabbed her handbag and raced to the door. At the last second, she took a red kerchief from a table and stuffed it into her shirt pocket. They ran to the coach just as the passengers boarded. Jason handed her some extra coins for train fare. She put the coins in her pocket, reached to hug him, then froze and stared behind him.

Jason turned to see Albert Danton and a clean-shaven ranch hand walking across the street. They walked around the front of the stagecoach. Danton looked Renée-Simone up and down with contempt.

"There's nowhere you can run, Renée," he said calmly, stepping up onto the boardwalk. To Jason he said, "You can't protect her once she leaves town. I'll have her back before sunset."

"I don't think so," Jason said. "I'll be with her."

"You're a wanted man, sir," Danton said smiling. "How long can you ride with her before the law finds out where you're headed? A day? Maybe two?"

Jason said nothing as he considered the logic of the man's reasoning while studying the bandage on Danton's left cheek.

"I'll have men waiting at the next town. Or the next, or the next after that. Not long after you've had to flee the law again, she'll be back here where she belongs. If I send out a wire, the Pinkertons will be back on your trail before the end of the day."

Jason quickly pulled his left holster gun before the ranch hand could react and pointed the weapon at Danton's chest. Three paces away, the stage driver saw the confrontation and slammed the coach door, then hurried away. Jason saw the four passengers cower below the edge of the half door as if the wood could protect them if bullets started flying. It was at that moment Jason realized what he'd just done. Without thinking, he'd put innocent people in danger.

Danton just shook his head. "I had a long talk with the Pinkerton detective who had to clean up the mess you made over in Franklin Town. You've got quite a reputation, but you're not a murderer." Danton clasped his hands behind his back.

"So grab your gun, and I can kill you with a clear conscience."

Jason nodded at the bulge that Danton's shoulder holster made under his suit jacket. He willed Danton to make a move for his gun, even a careless twitch that he could say triggered a gunfight, but the man made no hostile moves.

"I'll do no such thing."

Danton smiled as he called Jason's bluff. The mental battle continued. This time, Danton claimed victory.

"Think of it, Mr. Peares. If you kill an upstanding citizen of Kansas, one with wealthy connections, the governor's hunt for you will become even more intense. All to save a whore you don't even know."

"I'm not your whore," Renée-Simone said. Danton ignored her.

"Mister," the stage driver hollered to Jason from behind the coach. "I got a schedule to keep. Is the missy gettin' on?"

Jason looked from the driver to Danton, then back to the driver. He holstered his gun and shook his head. The driver climbed quickly into his seat, released the brake, and whipped his horses into a run. Jason and Danton stared at each other as the dust from the stage's fast departure settled around them.

"You can't save her. The best thing you can do for her is ride out. I'll forget the whole issue. She won't be punished. You have my word on that."

Though he gave no outward indication of his feelings, Jason felt only contempt for Danton and the honor of his promise. Maybe she wouldn't be punished, but she'd be Danton's slave, his high-priced saloon girl, until he said otherwise. Jason found that course of action unacceptable. He was just about to say so when he was interrupted by a familiar youthful voice to his right.

"Jason Peares, I'm calling you out!"

CHAPTER 10

J ASON TURNED SIDEWAYS AND LOOKED at the blond kid from Franklin Town. He stood on the boardwalk with his left hand flexing near a low-slung holster. It was a different rig than he'd worn last time Jason saw him. That guy who'd smacked him with a hat had probably taken his other gun belt away from him, like a parent would take away a child's favorite toy.

"I heard you were here, so I hurried over to visit."

"You heard I was here?"

"That's right. I can take you, and I aim to prove it."

Still facing the young gunfighter, Jason glanced back at Danton. He only had one weapon to use on the kid—his right gun. The other he had to keep free in case Danton or his ranch hand made a move. Sometimes if he thought his opponent was real fast, he'd flinch one hand and draw with the other, but facing the kid sideways didn't allow it this time. Besides, he had the distinct impression the kid was more bluster than capable.

As he mentally prepared himself, he saw Bonnie Drake step out of a store on the far side of the stagecoach office holding a rather large bag of goods. She looked casually off to the right, then to the left toward him. Her eyes lit up when she saw him. She opened her mouth to speak but froze when she saw the young gunfighter flexing only three paces in front of her.

Instead of ducking back inside for safety, Bonnie quickly put down her goods. Jason saw a small handbag draped from the crook of her left elbow and saw her reach in and pull out a gun.

No, don't be a hero!

She took one silent step forward, then a second, and Jason tried to keep the kid distracted.

"What's your name, kid? I always like to know who I'm killin'." Jason shrugged, stalling. He didn't want Bonnie caught in the cross fire.

"You ain't killin' nobody today. My name's Stanley Comb," the young man said smugly. "The man who killed Jason Peares."

Bonnie Drake took another silent step. Danton and his ranch hand backed into the street out of the line of fire.

"Well, before you kill me, tell me how is it you heard I was here?" Jason asked.

Comb opened his mouth to speak. Bonnie took her final step, arched her right arm up behind her head, and brought it swiftly down in front, like she was throwing a ball. She bounced her gun butt hard on the left side of Stanley Comb's skull, then flipped the gun deftly in her palm and had the young man covered before he hit the boardwalk. He didn't move. He was out cold.

Bonnie looked up and smiled at Jason, looking very pleased with her handiwork. She started to put her gun away but stopped as Jason stared at her, eyes narrowed. First, he looked at the boy's limp form on the boardwalk. Then he shifted his gaze to Bonnie and her gun as he considered the impossible.

Jason looked around frantically, seeking the trap he was absolutely certain was closing around him. Yet he found no concealed gunmen peering around the edges of stores. No riflemen sighted at him from the rooftops, behind false fronts.

Danton stood silently, calmly, hands behind his back. His ranch hand stood to his right, eyes twitching. Jason looked back at Bonnie and looked at her gun again.

Suddenly, he realized why her weapon bothered him. He stared at Bonnie, searching for answers, and found confirmation in her eyes at the same moment she must have seen his decision to act. He drew his right gun even as she began to jerk her arm forward to aim at him. She froze staring into the business end of his gun, her own weapon not quite aimed at him.

He kept his gaze on Bonnie. Didn't dare look away. She had her gun almost lined up with his head for a kill shot. Another slight arm movement and she'd shoot. Or he would.

Jason sensed movement to his left even before Renée-Simone gasped. He drew his left gun and fired without looking. He heard the rancher grunt and stumble backward, then heard the man and his gun flop into the dirt street. Still, he kept his concentration on Bonnie Drake.

She made no move as he stepped over to her. He holstered his left gun and pressed the barrel of his other against her forehead. She trembled slightly as he grabbed her weapon.

She matched his gaze. There were no pretenses here, Jason realized. He tilted his head slightly as he studied her eyes, trying to find the truth. His gut told him he was right about her. She handled her gun like a professional, had flipped it smoothly in her grip after spanking the kid upside the head.

"What was he going to say that you didn't want me to hear?"

She could have simply diffused the confrontation by sticking a gun to Comb's back. Instead, she'd silenced him. Now, she said nothing. She just stared at him but not with the panicked gaze of a nighttime saloon girl with a gun at her head. She was focused and calm.

With his thumb and forefinger, he pulled the pin under the barrel of her gun and shook open the cartridge, dumping the shells out. He dropped the gun, then reached for her handbag and upended it, dumping the contents to the boardwalk. When he looked down, he saw what he expected. A tin badge glittered in the sunlight. A Pinkerton detective's badge.

Jason turned his attention to Albert Danton, then walked over and pushed aside the flap of the man's suit coat with the tip of his gun. With his left hand, he pulled Danton's gun out of the holster strapped under his arm pit. He examined the well-used weapon, a small .32-caliber gun.

"Get yourself a real gun, Mr. Danton," Jason said. "You can't hurt nobody with this unless you accidentally shoot 'em in the eye."

He looked at Danton's ranch hand sitting on his rump off the boardwalk. The man glared back at Jason, holding a blood-soaked kerchief to his right collar. Jason eyed his gun, a dirty Colt .45 worn by cowboys and ranch hands all over the frontier. These men weren't Pinkertons.

Jason emptied Danton's gun and the rancher's, then backed away. He pulled a stunned Renée-Simone into the space between the general store and the stage office, intending to lead her back to his horse. He paused and glared at Bonnie Drake.

"I see you again, Miss, I'll shoot you without asking any questions. You hear me?"

She nodded, and Jason and Renée-Simone ran around back of the stage office and mounted up. They raced through alleys and side roads to the northwest edge of town.

"Where are we going?"

"Out there." He pointed ahead to the vast open range. "Where Danton will never find you. Where the Pinkertons will have a hard time finding me."

"I thought she was my friend," Renée-Simone said. "How did you know she's a deputy?"

Jason shook his head. "Not a deputy. She's a Pinkerton detective. Hauled that gun out of her handbag and twirled it around like a pro. I know guns fairly well, and hers was brand new. Heck, it was so clean I could see the gun metal gleaming from ten paces away. Still had that oily smell, too, when I examined it. Probably right out of the packing crate. She likely never even fired it."

"So?"

"It was a Schofield short-barrel .45 caliber. A favorite of big-city police and constables, especially in Chicago where I heard the Pinkerton Agency has its headquarters. Besides, even if a saloon girl could afford one, where would she buy a brand-new police gun around here?"

He thought for a moment. "Only one way that kid could've known I was there. He was on his way to Salina on other errands last night and chanced upon one of the detectives I saw in the saloon." Jason nodded as the pieces of the puzzle fell into place.

"Bonnie signaled them as soon as she saw me. Got them to leave and then made it look like she saved me, only so I would trust her. She just didn't want gunplay in a room full of people or out on the street where innocents might get hurt. That's against Pinkerton rules. I should've known something was wrong when she said they were riding out at night. Really, they were probably waiting to bushwhack me outside town."

Jason nodded as another thought occurred to him. "She kept trying to get me to go to the Hotel Salina, either to her room with her or to the dining room. If I had, then someone would have gone out and told the Pinkertons.

"Yeah, that's where they would've got me. Just good luck getting involved with you and Danton when I did. We lost them in the darkness, and they must've figured we snuck out during the night. They're still out scouting for my tracks. That's why Bonnie didn't have help back there."

Renée-Simone was silent as they rode. "I can't imagine the Pinkertons hiring women, especially not for such dangerous work."

Jason grunted. "A man's at his weakest with a woman."

"Or his strongest."

"Maybe," he conceded. "But he's only at his strongest with the right woman. Besides, more times than not, women can get close to their targets. They can get information men could never hope to get. I've heard the women in the Pinkerton Agency are every bit as well trained as the men. Some are even sharpshooters. And what better disguise is there than a saloon girl? She sees everybody that comes into town, knows everything about everyone."

"But she works for Mr. Danton. Does that mean he's one too?"

"No, he's definitely not a Pinkerton. I can see that when I

look into his eyes. He wants power. His hold over you isn't about money. It's about control. Bonnie used Danton as part of her cover story."

"Now that I think about it, I never actually saw her take a customer to her hotel room. But she always had money to pay Mr. Danton in the morning."

"Whatever detective she was reporting to would give her money to pay Danton. She'd never take customers to bed just to keep from being discovered." He thought for a few minutes.

"Did you ever see her meeting with anyone? Did she have any other friends, maybe someone you thought was courting her?"

"I don't think so. She spent most of her time at my house for the last month. She took to looking out for me like I was special to her. But really she was just using me, wasn't she, to cover her investigation?"

Jason nodded. "I've heard that Pinkertons have some really high standards they have to operate by. They care a lot about innocent victims and casualties and such. Maybe she took a liking to you because she knows what kind of man Danton is. Maybe she wanted to help you while she went about her other work."

"Finding you?"

"Yeah. Would've had me too, if not for that gun. I'm sure glad that kid showed up when he did. Else I would never have known it was Bonnie Drake who would have shot me in the back."

Even as he considered the turn of events, he still felt things seemed to fit together a little too perfectly. There were too many coincidences. Bonnie Drake could not possibly have known he was going to the saloon in Salina the night before. He'd only found the town by accident. By all rights, he should have been back near Franklin Town.

He realized, at that moment, the detectives from the Pinkerton Agency must have woven an intricate plot to capture him. They had studied him well, and their plans held many contingencies.

Three weeks ago, Bonnie and her group knew he would either visit Franklin Town or avoid it, so they were no doubt prepared for either choice he made. The gunfight had confused Jason, though. It seemed out of character for professional hunters until he realized Sanderville had made it personal.

Regardless, the Pinkertons had planned for the possibility that he would survive the subsequent manhunt through the flats west of Franklin Town. To be thorough, they were prepared for him to backtrack and visit Salina. Detectives were probably waiting for him in Franklin Town as well. They'd also have to consider the possibility that he might avoid either town. That meant they would be prepared to quickly regroup and pursue him.

Now Renée-Simone Fouché was in the picture. She would slow him down, too, tiring his horse with her added weight. He had to get her to a train as soon as possible. Somewhere far enough away Danton couldn't find her and the Pinkertons couldn't find him.

Jason nearly thought himself up a headache trying to consider all the possibilities. The Pinkertons would take action, but it would be carefully planned action. They'd follow his trail, also sending men to every nearby town in case they lost him. They'd spread their trackers so they could cross his trail quickly if he backtracked this time. Even if they didn't know exactly where he was, they'd try to keep him contained, giving him a limited number of possible escape routes.

Jason remained undaunted. He had survived the worst that man and nature could throw at him. Once he saw to the Frenchwoman's safety, he'd disappear in the vast emptiness of the wild frontier.

For a while, he had a traveling companion—a friend to keep away the loneliness. She was someone like himself, an outcast looking for somewhere to belong.

"Renée-Simone," he muttered to himself. The name had a nice sound about it.

"I heard you." She hugged him again, then shouted to the empty landscape. "I'm free!"

Jason found the stream again. He dropped his kerchief in to float downstream and rode upstream, leaving a short length of careless tracks along the banks of the stream. The Pinkertons would find the tracks and the kerchief, but with two such obvious possibilities, they wouldn't know which way to go. Maybe they might second-guess themselves, thinking they'd learned a lesson from his deception over the previous weeks.

They rode late into the evening, finally finding the main river that fed their stream and several others. Jason knew the Pinkertons didn't have enough men to cover the river and all the streams that fed it. Tomorrow, he'd choose a direction and they'd ride in the water all day. They'd never be found.

Jason set up camp shortly after sundown. Renée-Simone stared at him across the small fire as he prepared a simple dinner of beans and his last piece of salted beef steak in a tin skillet. He had no plates, so they both shared the grub out of the skillet with a single spoon. Afterward, they washed their food down with strong coffee.

The shirt and pants he'd grabbed for her in the store dwarfed her slender body. She was still very pretty, especially with her hair bundled up under her wide-brimmed hat. Her seductive voice and heavy French accent were no less enticing than the night before.

Something still nagged at him, though. Bonnie Drake's deceit was still fresh in his mind. No way a man could have gotten close to him the way the Pinkerton woman had. He shifted his gaze to the Frenchwoman as he suddenly realized the same conclusion could be made about Renée-Simone.

Then he shifted his gaze down to her breast pocket where the smallest of details had been bothering him since they stopped to camp. He often trusted his life to noticing such things, and now he saw that the little red kerchief he'd seen earlier no longer stuck out of her breast pocket.

"You don't trust me, do you?" she said.

"I stay alive by not trusting people. Where's your kerchief?"

"What?" She looked genuinely confused.

"The one that was in your shirt pocket earlier. Where is it?"

Renée-Simone paused for a long moment, then a look of hurt

feelings spread across her face. She reached into her front pants pocket and retrieved the wad of rag. Tossed it into Jason's lap.

"I had to use it, okay?"

Jason grabbed the rag, felt the wetness of the bundled cloth. He handed it back to her.

"I'm real sorry."

"It's okay. I guess you didn't see me blow my nose when we dismounted."

Jason shook his head and shrugged. "A lot has happened today. I'm just trying to figure it all out, that's all."

"Well, maybe I can explain everything to you."

Jason froze as he started to sip more coffee. The woman who sat before him was a completely different person than the one he'd briefly come to know. Her seductive French accent vanished in her last statement, along with the demure look in her eyes. A mischievous smile flashed across her face, and confidence replaced vulnerability.

He looked over the rim of his metal cup as Renée-Simone reached into her purse. When she pulled her hand out, he saw she held a brand-new Schofield, short-barrel six-gun. A Pinkerton weapon.

CHAPTER II

"**D**AMN!" JASON SHOOK HIS HEAD. "You played me like a fiddle."

"I understand why you don't trust people, Jason. It probably keeps you alive."

"I suppose your name isn't Renée-Simone?" She shook her head. "Well," he said, "how long have you been a Pinkerton detective?"

Again she shook her head. "Blackmailer and thief."

Jason raised an eyebrow in surprise.

"Renée Shelley is my real name." When she paused, Jason got the feeling she expected him to know about her. He shrugged and she continued.

"Well, maybe you've heard of my brother, Tom Shelley? He's quite famous back East. Or maybe I should say notorious."

Jason shook his head. "I don't get back East much. Don't know the name."

"I'm hurt," she said, smiling. Renée reversed the gun in her hand and tossed it to Jason. He caught it and checked the chamber. It was full. He handed the weapon back.

"I'm not your enemy, Jason."

"Obviously."

She put the gun back in her handbag. "I'd been working some towns all over Kansas, befriending wealthy ranchers or cattle owners or businessmen. Always the married ones. We'd meet for a rendezvous, have dinner and drinks. Just when a man thought he was going to get lucky, I'd pull a gun and relieve him of his jewelry and money.

"What could they do?" She shrugged. "They couldn't report me, right? They'd have to explain why they were meeting with me. Then their wives would hear about it. If they were really rich, I'd blackmail them and threaten to tell lies to their wives or business partners. They'd happily go straight to the bank and withdraw money for me, just to keep me quiet. Then I'd disappear. I had a perfect setup going."

"Except the Pinkertons caught you."

She nodded. "I learned later one of the men I swindled had some pretty high political connections. I didn't even know the Pinkertons were onto me. Bonnie Drake and Albert Danton caught me over in Dodge City." She chuckled as Jason again betrayed his surprise.

"Danton?"

She nodded. "He's the area chief for all the Midwest."

"Damn!"

"They pulled the same ruse on me. She's the saloon girl, and he's the manager. He pretended to be married. When I tried to get him to meet with me, he suggested a naughty three-way with Bonnie. I figured she and I could split the loot and she could buy her freedom, but they just arrested me. They were taking me back to Kansas City for trial when they got the news about two months ago that you were in the territory.

"Danton offered me my freedom if I helped them capture you. I was supposed to get close to you so you'd rescue me from Franklin Town."

"No, that doesn't make sense. They had me surrounded."

"They figured you wouldn't shoot up the place to escape, but they didn't want to take the chance of innocent people getting hurt. I was supposed to be the helpless French maiden. After I got close to you, they'd act like I was a hostage and let you leave. I'd leave a trail, and they'd surround you out in the open."

Jason didn't speak for a while. "I can't believe the Pinkerton

National Detective Agency would allow its agents to put a hostage in a dangerous situation like that."

"Jason." Renée paused as if considering what to say. She crawled around the fire and sat next to him. She looked into his eyes and said, "Albert Danton knows everything about you. He has detailed notes."

She touched his arm. "He knew you wouldn't turn away from someone in need. That's why they wanted me to be needy, vulnerable. They knew you wouldn't hurt me."

Jason tossed the rest of his lukewarm coffee into the fire and fiddled with the metal cup. "Then why the gun? To shoot me in the back?"

Renée shook her head. "Danton gave me the gun just in case he was wrong about you. I told him I never shot anyone before, but he made me keep it anyway."

Jason nodded and gazed at the burning sticks. He'd been as predictable as a child, escaping in the end only because of a lucky twist of fate. "But why stage the gunfight in Franklin Town? Doesn't fit their rules."

"That wasn't supposed to happen. But Sanderville and his men disobeyed Danton's orders. I guess Sanderville's pride got the better of his judgment. They thought they could take you."

Jason disagreed. "One of Sanderville's kinfolk came looking for me a while back, and I killed him."

Renée nodded. "I didn't know about that. Anyway, Danton was furious. He said later that it took all of his self-control not to shoot you in the back after you gunned down his men."

"Good thing he didn't try. After a gunfight, when my heart's beating fast and furious, I'm really primed and aware of everything around me. I heard him start to make his play. I would've shot him dead on the spot."

"He said as much after you left town."

Jason considered her explanation. "How did he know I would escape the posse and double back?"

"He said he'd been studying you even before the governor requested the Pinkerton Agency to take the case. He talked to other lawmen that have tracked you. Figured you might outrun the posse. Said doubling back was your style. But he didn't think you'd go back to Franklin Town, so he set up operations in Salina."

"Just dumb luck, then," Jason said. "Franklin Town was exactly where I was headed. I only found Salina quite by accident."

He thought for a moment. "Bonnie saw me come into the saloon, signaled the other Pinkertons, and got your attention. Then you folks started your performance."

Jason suddenly wanted more coffee. He set the cup aside and placed the pot back on the glowing embers of the fire. Renée continued her story.

"We'd been waiting at the saloon every night for almost three weeks. All that time on the run, a man's gonna get tired of not knowing how extensive the net is. I'd pretend to be forced into whoring. Turn down my first customer, Mr. Billings—he's a detective too. The original plan from Franklin Town was to try to get you to be sympathetic and rescue me."

Jason reflected on Danton's plan, amazed at its complexity. "He had a contingency for every action I might take." Renée nodded. "I thought Bonnie was a real saloon girl, what with that kiss and all."

"You kissed her?"

"Twice. Well, she did most of the kissing. I just kinda stood there." He chuckled.

"Sure you did." She punched him lightly on the arm. "Is she a good kisser?"

"I reckon." He fell silent for a while. "Danton had damn near a perfect plan," Jason admitted.

"Except for that gunfighter showing up when he did."

"Yeah." Jason nodded. "Stanley Comb's got me worried. If he's on my trail, sooner or later he'll find me again. I think he's got something to prove. He thinks he can outdraw me. They always do."

"Like the Pinkertons, he's got to find us first."

"Us?"

"Of course," Renée said. "Don't you see? I'm free, but I didn't have to deliver you."

"Yeah, I'm sure you're already back on Danton's criminal list."

"Like I said, he has to find me. Who better to travel with than the outlaw Jason Peares?"

Jason started to speak but hesitated. He looked at Renée, at her devilish smile. Then the truth struck him. He raised his eyebrows in surprise.

"You didn't just betray Danton. You beat him at his own game while his mind was on catching me."

She nodded. "He's too smart for his own britches. Always bragging on how much he studied you, how much he admired your skill and accomplishments. Thinking up all these grandiose plans."

Renée waved a hand around as if to trivialize Danton's plans. She kept smiling, obviously very pleased with herself. She leaned in and kissed him. Her breath tasted like coffee. Hers was a different kind of kiss than Bonnie's. It was less a physical performance than an intimate probe into his soul, and he was deeply disappointed when she pulled away.

"After everything they told me about you, I knew somehow you'd find a way to escape. All I had to do was convince you to take me with you. I never intended to leave them a trail." Renée paused and looked at Jason for a moment. "I'm sorry that I used you, but I needed you alive for my own escape. And now I need you to keep me alive."

CHAPTER 12

T WO WEEKS PASSED, THEN TWO months, then four. They made slow progress, resting the horse frequently and always moving west and north, away from Kansas and away from the Pinkertons. Jason used every trick he knew to cover their trail.

Jason and Renée grew closer, and what surprised him was how easy it was to let her into his life. A loner by nature, he often avoided getting close to people to prevent the inevitable disappointment. More than once, Jason had tasted the bitter pill of a friendship betrayed.

Renée was different. She understood what his last few years on the run had been like. More importantly, she had no need for the bounty she might get by turning him in. He wasn't sure what exactly she needed beyond his protection and companionship, but they fit well together on the trail. He felt as though she belonged with him, and he grew to appreciate that feeling more and more as each day passed. He enjoyed having her in his life.

After the first month, Jason walked his horse more each day. He fed and watered it as much as possible, sometimes letting it rest several days at a time. He never knew when they'd need to ride hard, so he kept the mount fresh and strong.

During the daytime, Jason and Renée avoided all towns that might have a telegraph line, figuring the Pinkertons had wired notices around to watch for them. They ate what Jason hunted, and they traded extra meat for potatoes, vegetables, and other necessities when they came across other travelers or homestead-ers. Every now and again, they put in at the camps of cattle drivers or slept in barns of friendly farmers or ranchers.

Eventually, Jason and Renée rode through the early snows in eastern Colorado. Then they fled south for Texas before winter arrived in full strength. They always avoided well-traveled trails, and sometimes they saw not a soul for weeks at a time. Jason knew Albert Danton and Bonnie Drake wouldn't quit, but the cowboy detectives would be hard-pressed to strike any hint of their trail.

In the northern part of Texas, Jason found an abandoned one-room cabin on the banks of a narrow stream just east of the New Mexico border. They settled in for the winter, and he rounded up a couple dozen unbranded longhorns to trade for supplies. They lived an isolated existence many miles from any-thing resembling a town.

Winter passed peacefully and without event. Still, one of Jason's biggest concerns was whether or not Renée would be able to hold her own in a conflict if trouble ever caught up with them. He expressed his fear one chilly morning over coffee by the fireplace.

"I want to teach you how to shoot."

"I've never had much need for shooting," she said. "I was born and raised back East where we had civilization. There wasn't much need for a lady to handle guns."

"Sooner or later someone will come calling after me. You may get caught up in it, and I'd feel much better if you could handle a pistol fairly well or shoot a Winchester with reasonable accuracy. That skill might save your life."

Jason continued to pick up a few wild horses and cattle, and they settled into a routine that represented what Jason thought life should be like. Through the months, there were no gunfights or chases or adventures. They just lived a peaceful existence alone on the frontier, bothered by no one, day after uneventful day.

After a particularly long and grueling day of carving up a

beef, smoke-cooking some, and salting the rest for preservation, Jason went to the river to bathe in the frigid water. Renée sent him back twice more to wash the smell away.

When he finally trudged back up to the cabin shivering, Renée had a huge bowl of steaming beef and vegetable stew waiting to thaw him. After supper, they sat on a log in front of the cabin, holding hands as they watched the sun set. A small bonfire burned, relaxing them with its constant crackle, hypnotizing them with its dancing flames, and warming them with its heat.

"Life doesn't get much better than this," Jason said.

He was as settled as he could ever hope to be. No one pursued him, at least not that he knew about at that particular moment. Maybe even the Pinkerton Agency had given up the chase.

While he hadn't seen his friend and shadow, trouble, for several months, he knew it would likely show its ugly face when he began to feel complacent. For now, he was happy and said as much.

"And I've got a wonderful, sweet woman to keep me company. Did I mention how beautiful you are?"

She smiled. "Do you ever wish for more?"

He looked at her and squeezed her hand. Her light brown eyes shone in the waning sun and sparkled in the firelight. He nodded.

"I often dream about finding a ranch or farm someplace where no one has ever heard of Jason Peares."

She sighed, looked away. "It's time for you to go, isn't it? You're going to leave me."

"No," he said quickly. He squeezed her hand again. "But when it's time to go, I'm hoping you'll go with me."

She turned toward him and touched his cheek. "Do you ever think about getting married? Maybe having children?"

Jason recovered from his surprise quickly. Stared deep into her eyes a moment. Sure, he'd thought about it, but only as a fantasy.

What kind of life could he offer a woman? How could he drag

a family across the land every time a lawman or a bounty hunter set out on his trail? Worse, when someone finally caught up with him and killed him, his family would be left without a father or husband. He couldn't outshoot everyone forever. Sooner or later, someone better or faster would come along. Or he'd get caught unsuspecting in an ambush.

He started to speak, then he realized what Renée was telling him. He nodded in understanding.

"It's time for *you* to go, isn't it?"

"No!" she said. "Jason, I love you. I'm not gonna run away." She seemed embarrassed at that disclosure. "I'm sorry," she said after a moment. "I didn't mean to say that." She sat in silence awhile.

"It's just that I'll be twenty-five soon and, well, a girl needs more." She paused again, then continued. "I never stayed in one place for long after my mama died. I just drifted a lot. Got pretty good at relieving men of their valuables." She chuckled. "With that kind of skill, I had to keep moving, you know?"

"I know exactly what you mean." Jason nodded. "Mostly, I work cattle drives to keep on the move. I haven't stayed put since I first left home seven years ago." He looked over at her again.

"I don't know exactly when I started loving you, Renée, but it's been awhile now. I'm just sorry I never said so before today."

She smiled and wiped a tear from her cheek. She reached for his hand and kissed his knuckles with a feathery touch of her soft lips.

"You seem like such a gentle person, not the man they say murdered an unarmed deputy."

Jason shook his head. "I never killed anyone who wasn't trying to kill me." He paused and looked at Renée, confused. "Danton tell you that?"

She nodded. "Your first gunfight in Malden, Missouri."

"Wasn't no deputy around. Just that bigoted sheriff who threw me in jail after I shot the men who..."

Jason's voice cracked, and he took a deep breath that ended with a shudder. Even after seven years, he'd never really taken the time to grieve over the loss of his family. He'd never cried about them. It hurt terribly, but he kept stuffing the pain deep inside where he wouldn't have to feel it.

Renée scooted closer and put her arm around his shoulder. "How did you become the outlaw everyone wants to kill? It doesn't seem fair."

Jason sifted through old memories. Only sixteen years old, he'd been sent out by his father into the Cumberland Forest to hunt game for their winter food supply. The next week, he returned to find his homestead burned-out. His family had been shot down like animals as they tried to escape the burning cabin.

Young Jason set out after the killers, not to kill them, for he was too young and naive to do such a thing. He wanted to have them arrested, so he tracked them to Malden, Missouri. There, as a sheltered boy from Kentucky, he had his first encounter with racism and frontier justice. The sheriff refused to help him and told him bluntly that no White men would hang on the word of a half-Black, half-White farm boy.

As he left town, the killers found him, and Jason learned his true calling. When the gun smoke cleared, four of the five killers lay dead in the street. Young Jason got himself arrested for murder. With help from a sympathetic witness, he'd escaped, but the sheriff put up a reward for his capture.

Though young and scared, Jason had an innate gift for gun handling. Still, he was losing the battle of survival before he was even twenty years old. About that time, he met a Chinese immigrant railroad worker named Liu Wang. The philosophical old man said he was journeying toward California to spend his final days gazing across the ocean toward the land he'd originally immigrated from.

Along the way, the old man taught Jason mental discipline and silent physical combat. He showed him how to use his brain more than his guns. He made the difference between death and survival for young Jason.

Over the years, Jason's bounty grew as hunters and lawmen tried to kill him. He had no defense against the sheriff's claims of murder. He knew he wouldn't get a fair trial, even if he could find any of the witnesses to the original shooting.

So he became a fugitive, an outlaw. He avoided trouble when he could, but when he couldn't flee, he fought back the only way he knew how. When lawmen or bounty hunters caught him and forced him into a gunfight, he killed them. He had no choice.

Jason continued to drift, always to another ranch or cattle trail. Sooner or later, someone would always hear about his latest gunfight. Maybe it would be a lawman or a bounty hunter. Most often, it would be kinfolk of someone he'd dispatched years before. They'd seek him out, and he'd dispatch them too. Then the chase would begin anew.

Renée turned toward him. "You didn't shoot an unarmed deputy in Malden?"

He shook his head. "I don't recall there being any deputies in that town to be shot, armed or otherwise. Just the men that killed my family. After that, the sheriff threw me down in the mud and arrested me."

"Truthfully?" she begged. He said nothing. "Please, Jason. This is important."

"The only men I shot were them that killed my family. They confessed as much right there on the spot. I just can't prove it. Nobody would listen anyway, not to me or any witnesses."

"Witnesses?" she said hesitantly. "There were witnesses?"

"Sure." Jason shrugged. "It was early evening, but it was still light out. Plenty of folks walking around saw the gunfight. The sheriff dragged me past them when he threw me in jail." He looked into the dancing flames. "Doesn't matter, though."

Renée pulled his arm, beckoning him to look at her. She stared at him for a long time. Her gazed danced back and forth from one eye to the other. Jason got the uncomfortable feeling she was trying to measure the truth in his words by eye contact. Finally, she turned away.

"Dear God, Jason. They've got it all wrong."

"The Pinkertons?"

She looked at him and nodded.

"Well, I've learned to live with the situation." He paused. "So, you can see I don't have much to offer a woman. Life with me will be pretty much as it was before we stopped here. We'd have to live fairly isolated so no one can find us. Maybe change our names too. Probably won't have any permanent friends or a homestead. If someone finds us, we'll have to pick up and leave everything and everyone behind. Sometimes we'll spend weeks or months on the trail until we're safe."

He paused to let his words sink in.

"Or you might be waiting up for me one night five months or five years from now, and someone will have found me and ended it."

"I know." Renée was silent for a while. "We could go down to Mexico?"

"That's where a lot of outlaws run to, thinking they'll be safe. I guarantee you that Danton has sent wires to all the sizable border towns to keep watch for us."

"How about Canada?"

"Pretty darn cold up there."

She rose suddenly, then reached down and practically hauled Jason to his feet.

"Okay, then we'll go to California. I've heard there are vast amounts of open land out there still unclaimed. No one will ever find us there."

Jason nodded and smiled. "When do you want to leave?"

"Tomorrow morning."

With that conclusion agreed to, Jason and Renée found themselves on the trail again, except this time they had a purpose. A month on the trail toward their new home found them heading northwest, crossing the border from New Mexico into Arizona just as winter cast its last breath across the Southwest. Cold winds and icy snow blew over the barren land. They needed to find shelter, a place to wait out the storm.

After the initial excitement of seeking a new home together in California, they had planned their departure poorly. They still had several mountain ranges to cross. The high snows that made the mountain trails impassable wouldn't melt for another couple of months.

Before leaving Texas, Jason had traded their livestock for a bridle-trained horse for Renée, the same breed as his own, and two pack mules loaded down with supplies for the long trip. Now their tiny caravan trudged slowly along a deeply rutted trail. They leaned forward against the freezing wind blowing snow horizontally against them. The animals struggled into the late winter storm, heads to the ground.

Jason and Renée wore thick leggings over their pants. Both had their sheepskin coats buttoned up to the neck, collars pushed up over their ears, noses, and mouths. Throat straps held their hats down tight.

Renée shouted against the howling wind and pointed off to the left at a cabin in the distance. They angled across the plain to find the cabin just an abandoned adobe shell, its rooms open to the sky. Jason led the animals into a side room so they'd be protected from the freezing wind. Renée started a fire in an old stove without a vent pipe.

Numb to the bone, they skipped supper. Instead, they cuddled together under blankets in front of the fire. When they awoke in the morning, their blankets and the floor covered with a thin dusting of snow, they found the sun halfway to noon, already melting the heavy snow outside the cabin.

When Jason walked outside, he saw a tiny town barely two miles away from their shelter. Had they continued riding in the storm, they would have ridden right past the town. Jason and Renée decided to search there for a hot breakfast.

As they rode in from the east, gunshots rang out in the crisp air. Jason knew his old friend, trouble, waited ahead for him.

CHAPTER 13

J ASON REACHED QUICKLY BEHIND HIM into his pack and pulled out his gun belt. He stood in his stirrups and, in less than a minute, had his two-gun rig belted around his waist, thigh straps securely tied. He sat back down and checked his Schofields, then he nodded to Renée to fall back behind him.

The place seemed too small to be called a town. There were seven small, flat-roofed, earth-colored adobe buildings. They passed the tiny boardinghouse first, on the left. A small stable sat out back and a decent-sized corral separated the boarding-house from the rest of the structures. Jason guessed the board-inghouse served a dual function as a stagecoach office, but it was probably just a quick stop along the road where the coach could get fresh horses.

After the corral and boardinghouse, the kitchen house and general store lined the left side of the road. The sheriff's office and a couple other buildings sat across the road. Jason figured the town was too small for a real sheriff or deputy. Likely, a self-appointed lawman was just official enough to let visitors know the law existed.

A tiny church sat a hundred paces up the road, on the right. Beyond the church, a dozen houses were scattered haphazardly across the land. In the distance, Jason could see a dried-up riv-erbed, bordered by tall cottonwoods barren of leaves. He guessed the river water flowed beneath the ground.

Two men stumbled out of the kitchen house as Jason rode

up the middle of the town's only dirt road. His horse clopped noisily in the muddy slush caused by the snow melt. The rise of each hoof made a wet sucking sound followed by a squishing splash.

Three motley-looking troublemakers followed the two victims into the road, surrounding them. They waved the business ends of their guns at the men and pushed them to their knees in the mud. They made them beg for their lives.

A fourth ruffian slammed open the kitchen house door and stomped out into the mud. Jason instantly knew this man led the group. He would determine the fate of the two elderly men being humiliated in the mud.

A bear of a man, he wore only an undershirt in the brisk morning cold while his partners all wore heavy overcoats. The top of his head showed a crown of bare skin. Shoulder-length black hair formed a ring around the side of his head from one ear to the other.

The leader barked an order, and one of his men kicked a hostage in the back. The man fell face down in the mud. From thirty paces, Jason saw a glint of sunlight off metal on the man's coat. The sheriff wiped mud from his face as he struggled back to his knees.

The leader of the ruffians bellowed laughter, his giant belly shaking with the effort. He didn't seem to notice Jason's approach. The man tossed a handgun into the mud, then taunted the sheriff to pick it up and draw. The leader already had his gun drawn.

Jason pulled both guns as he approached.

"Hey, mister," he said. Two of the ruffians were forced to step aside as Jason guided his horse close behind the sheriff and the other hostage. "I don't take kindly to bullies. First one of you moves a gun toward me, I'm gonna start shootin'."

"This ain't none of your concern."

"You fellows can either stash those guns and ride out, or you can use them." The troublemakers hesitated, then glanced at each other. "And don't think too long about it, either."

The leader squinted his eyes. Jason knew he was measuring his odds of escaping the shootout alive with Jason already pointing a gun at his head. The man finally nodded and holstered his gun.

He backed away and his men followed him up the street to get their horses tied up in front of the boardinghouse. Jason saw Renée covering them with a Winchester as she rode past them.

The sheriff got to his feet and made a show of wiping mud from his face with his coat sleeve as he turned toward Jason. The other man, older and heavier, white-haired, ran straight for the kitchen house door.

"I'm obliged to you, son," the sheriff said. He found a dry patch on his right pant leg and wiped mud from his hand. He reached up for a handshake. Jason holstered his guns and leaned down to return the gesture.

"I'm Vern Hamilton, and if there's anything I can do for you, just name it."

Sheriff Hamilton had serious, steel-gray eyes and silver hair. He stood tall but not so straight. Jason guessed he was on the far side of sixty. He saw recognition in Hamilton's eyes.

Jason dismounted beside the sheriff. "You know who I am."

Hamilton nodded. "I know who you are, son. Just got the new poster in the mail pouch last month."

"I don't want any trouble, sir. I'll be on my way."

"Well, first let's get some grub into ya," Hamilton said. "I'm alive to do so on account of you." He nodded behind Jason as Renée walked her horse up. "And for the lady too, if she's hungry."

"Kind of you, Sheriff," Jason said hesitantly.

"I know what you're thinking, son." Hamilton wrapped his arm friendly-like around Jason's shoulder and led him toward the kitchen. "Ten thousand dollars is more money than an old dawg like me ever seen. But I don't figure I got enough years left to spend it all."

Hamilton chuckled as they entered the dining room. Without a boardwalk to scrape their boots on, they tracked mud onto the floor. Jason held the door as Renée entered behind him. He whispered to her.

"Bounty's up to ten thousand now."

Her eyes widened in surprise. Jason had figured his bounty would increase after his encounter with the Pinkerton detectives, but he'd never guessed it would jump so much. Before Salina and Franklin Town, he was only worth $7,000. He now had the distinction of being the highest-priced outlaw in history, as far as he knew.

Two men greeted them. The younger of the two had his right sleeve torn away. A bloodsoaked rag covered what Jason guessed was a bullet graze on his upper arm. The other man had spent time kneeling in the mud beside Hamilton.

Jason introduced Renée to Vince Parsons and his son Frank, and then introduced himself only as Jay. After the two Parsons men left, the three took one of the tables closest to the door.

"In my younger days, I sure wouldn't have let any young punks come in here and disarm me, not without making a fight of it anyway."

Jason smiled. "Ever think about retiring, Sheriff?"

Hamilton wiped more mud from his face and flung it to the floor.

"Hell, I'm about as retired as a man can be in these parts and still be useful for something." Jason nodded as a heavyset woman walked over and placed their food in front of them.

"It was cooked earlier, but I kept it warm," she said.

Renée smiled at her. "I'm sure it will be delicious."

They tore into their food as Hamilton continued to talk. Jason suspected talking was something the old man liked to do. He didn't mind, though. After so many weeks on the trail, Jason and Renée at times rode for hours in complete silence, not being able to think up new topics for small talk.

"We don't get much excitement around here. I can't recall the last time a famous person passed through. But don't you worry none, young man. We're a friendly folk hereabouts. Won't cause you no trouble, so stay as long as you're of a mind to."

Jason nodded. "What's this place called?" he said with a mouth full of hard-fried eggs and potatoes.

"We're much too small to be on any map, but we call ourselves Greenville, on account of a big swatch of wild grass over the river. Imagine that. Right in the middle of a desert." Hamilton chuckled and continued. "It ain't green yet, but it will be in a month or so.

"We got us some Indian activity up north, so be careful if you're headed thataway. There's only a handful of families around here. The Parsons own a ranch out yonder and the Bellevues run the only farm around. It's only a thousand acres.

"Come to think of it, I bet Vince could use an extra hand, if you're thinkin' about settlin' in for a bit."

Jason looked at Renée and she nodded. He said, "Maybe until the snows melt off a bit up north."

"Well, you'll be needin' a place to stay, then."

Renée chuckled. "We borrowed someone's cabin over yonder." She looked at the sheriff. "Be nice if we could find a place with a roof, though."

Hamilton laughed a snorting nasal kind of sound. "My son has a cabin about three miles northeast of here. Never cared much about living down here with the rest of us. Went up to Colorado to do some hunting. I won't be seeing him again until summer, at the earliest."

Jason nodded. "We'll be long gone by then, but we're grateful for your hospitality."

"Good. It's settled then." Hamilton stood. "I'm going over to check on Frank, and I'll speak to Vince about hiring you. His wife owns the general store, Miss. Maybe she might need some extra help too."

"That'll be just fine," Renée said. She leaned against Jason and wrapped her arm around his neck. "But we won't be staying long. I'm taking him to California where we might find a preacher who will marry us."

"That's wonderful," Hamilton said. "Anything else I can do for you folks?"

Jason nodded. "You could let me know if any strangers come around looking for us."

Renée and Jason settled into the younger Hamilton's cabin in the hills, beyond town. Jason took a job with Mr. Parsons tending horses and doing farm work, while Renée stacked jars and bundles of food and other supplies on shelves for the very likable Mrs. Parsons. The pleasant woman never seemed to mind Renée's extended breaks when Jason came around.

Two months passed before they finally talked about marriage again and about moving on toward California. Jason brought up the topic, though in a man's kind of way.

Where would they live? Who would marry them? What would they do if someone found him? What if someone found her? How many children did she want?

Renée had no answers and instead said she didn't care about what or how or why. All she wanted was to be with him. Forever.

Jason smiled and hummed to himself as he rode into town one Sunday morning, reliving the conversation. He left Renée at the cabin, begging that he had to make a special purchase for her. She tried to guess what he was buying, but he kept the secret.

He rode straight for the fabric store where he was going to have Mrs. Smith, the owner, make a dress from a bundle of silk material he'd seen in her store. Renée hadn't owned a dress since leaving Kansas. He knew she'd be overjoyed getting a silk dress for a gift.

As he dismounted, he heard a whistle behind him, across the street. He turned and saw Sheriff Hamilton waving at him. The sheriff closed his office door and walked fast in Jason's direction.

"What's new, Sheriff?" Jason said as he met him in the middle of the wide street.

"You wanted to know if any strangers came around?" Jason nodded, suddenly wary, and the sheriff continued. "There's some people rode in just last night."

"Looking for me?"

Hamilton shook his head. "No, actually, they asked about

your lady friend. Been showing a sketch around. Except they're calling her by another name."

Hamilton stroked his beard thoughtfully. Jason narrowed his eyes.

"Not Renée Shelley?"

"No. They inquired about her using a French name."

At first, Jason thought one of her past victims might have finally found her, though he didn't see how that was possible after almost a year.

"Renée-Simone Fouché?"

"Yeah, that's it. There's two of 'em. A handsome, big-bosomed woman and a southern gentleman."

Jason narrowed his eyes. Albert Danton and Bonnie Drake. Somehow, the Pinkerton Agency had found them. He looked down and examined a rut in the hardpacked dirt street, then kicked at the rut with the heel of his boot.

He had to get Renée to safety. Hopefully, they'd have enough time to pack supplies for the long chase. They'd have to leave everything else behind. Just as he'd promised, someone had found them, and now they had to run again. It was a hell of a life to share.

"Sheriff, I'm obliged to you, but somebody here must have sent word to the Pinkertons that we were here. That's the only way they could have found us. If they find out any of you have helped us, they'll be madder 'n hell. Could be a lot of trouble for you. Tell 'em I threatened you or that you didn't know who I was."

Hamilton nodded and they shook hands. Jason pivoted to his left and froze. Bonnie Drake stood in the doorway of the kitchen house. She was already pulling her hand out of her handbag. They locked stares.

Jason saw no panic in her eyes, only professional concentration. She opened her mouth as if to say something.

With an instinctive habit born of years of gun contests, Jason reached to draw his right holster gun. He slapped his hand against his pant leg and recalled he hadn't worn his gun belt for weeks.

He wasted no time cursing his error. Without hesitation, Jason swept his hand up and grabbed his belt gun. Even as he pulled it free, he heard another sound behind him, a palm slapping against a gun butt. Then he heard metal sliding against leather and knew the detectives had caught him in a cross fire.

In one fluid motion, Jason drew and snapped off a quick shot at Bonnie, then dropped and spun toward Danton. He and Danton fired at the same time, both shots missing. They both fired as fast as they could work their guns, and Jason knew the first man who scored would be the one who lived.

His gun empty, he watched Danton start to reload. Jason patted his pockets but had nothing to reload with. He thought about rushing the man, but Danton was too far away. He'd finish his reload before Jason could cover the distance.

Suddenly, the detective leaned back against the wall of the general store for support. Two blood stains spread in the center of his white shirt. The detective fumbled with his cartridges but dropped them. He awkwardly reached for more from a pocket, but Jason could see the man was critically wounded.

Jason walked over and kicked his feet out from under him. Danton slid down the wall and flopped on his rump. His suit jacket caught on a nail and got pulled up over his shoulders. He dropped his gun and started to fall over sideways, but the hooked jacket kept him partially upright. His eyes closed.

Jason scanned the seven buildings of Greenville, surprised not to see more Pinkerton detectives. He only saw ten people, including Bonnie Drake. The owner of the general store now stood in the doorway beside him. The pleasant proprietor of the kitchen house cautiously approached Bonnie's inert form. Jason's shot had knocked her against the kitchen doorway. She bounced off and ended up face down in the dirt.

Two other people watched from in front of the boardinghouse down the road. Five others filed out of the adobe church at the far west end of town. Then Jason saw the sheriff lying in the street, his neck a bloody mess. He walked over to the man and knelt beside him. The sheriff wasn't dead yet, but he was fading fast, eyes glazed in shock. The end was mercifully quick.

Jason removed his hat for a moment. He and Danton had thrown hot lead all over creation, and another innocent bystander had paid the price.

He looked over at Bonnie and saw her move. He walked over, surprised to see not a gun in her hand but a piece of paper. He stuck his foot against her left hip and roughly rolled her onto her back. She screamed and grabbed her side as he moved her. He knelt beside her and watched as she gasped quick, shallow breaths. She writhed in pain. He wanted her to suffer a long painful death.

Bonnie wore a high-necked, light blue cotton dress. Her flowery hat lay nearby. She wore a new disguise today in place of her saloon girl outfit. It was just as well since Greenville had no saloon. Maybe she was pretending to be Danton's wife.

Blood darkened her dress below her massive left breast, near her side. Jason fought back the bitter taste of disappointment. He could easily see it was a minor injury and she'd live. She screamed when he felt her back. He found the bloodsoaked hole in her dress. His bullet had passed straight through her side near the skin. As he suspected, it hadn't hit anything vital, though it might have grazed and bruised a rib. It probably hurt like hell, but she'd be up walking around tomorrow.

"Doesn't look good, Detective," he lied. He hated her for causing the death of a good man, for destroying his own peaceful life with his future wife. Bonnie had to suffer. She rocked her head back and forth, gritting her teeth against the pain.

Jason continued. "Looks to me like the bullet went right through your lung. I'll be surprised if you last until noon." He glanced up at the sun. "You've got a couple hours of pain left."

Bonnie turned her face toward him, focused her eyes on his. He looked down at her with his most intimidating, hate-filled gaze.

"Who told you we were here?" She said nothing. "Who told

you?" He grabbed her roughly by the chin, forced her not to turn away. "Where are the rest of your detectives?"

Bonnie was silent for a long time. Finally, she spoke.

"She's my sister."

CHAPTER 14

SQUATTING ON HIS HAUNCHES, JASON was stunned and almost lost his balance. He froze, unable to speak or even breathe. It seemed impossible, but as he gazed into Bonnie's eyes, he saw the truth in her words.

He released her jaw and moved his hand up, covering her nose and mouth so he could only see her eyes. She had the same light brown eyes Renée had. Bonnie Drake wasn't lying.

Hands grabbed him by the shoulders and nudged him gently, a suggestion to stand and move aside. He did so and moved away as an elderly man examined her wound. Then, the man told her the truth about the injury.

Jason spoke to Bonnie without looking at her. "What's her real name?"

Bonnie winced as the man cut away part of her dress.

"Shelley Drake."

"And she's a Pinkerton detective?"

Bonnie nodded with a grimace. Jason tried several times to speak, but he couldn't find the words. He simply walked over to his horse and busied himself with checking his Winchester and reloading his empty gun. Then he mounted up and rode over and stopped in front of the kitchen. He looked down at Bonnie.

"You and your posse are going to regret ever taking up my trail. I'm through running from you. You better tell them boys to go back home to their families while they're still able." He paused. "That lying sister of yours is going to pay long and hard.

Then I'm coming after you and the rest of your men. Anyone who wants to keep breathing ought not be here when I get back."

He turned his horse away, but Bonnie called after him, "Jason, don't kill her!"

Jason rode away as Bonnie screamed his name. She wailed in pain as she tried to move, imploring him not to hurt her sister. He ignored her. The truth was he could no sooner kill the woman he loved than he could shoot himself in the head.

He let Bonnie think the worst, though. She needed to suffer for the death of the sheriff, a man whose only crime was befriending Jason and standing in the wrong place at the wrong moment.

He saw everything so clearly now, but he realized the clues had been right in front of him all along. Renée had fabricated lie after lie. She had manipulated him like a child. She'd used him until she could contact Danton and Bonnie.

From their escape out of Salina, she'd played on his weaknesses and observed his actions. Then she had adapted, telling him exactly what he needed to hear to believe her. She knew he wanted to believe her. When he asked her about the missing kerchief, she knew he was suspicious. It was obvious he would watch her closely, maybe look through her purse and find the gun. So she gave it to him voluntarily to gain his trust. Then she concocted the perfect story about being a thief. It was something he could identify with, even sympathize with. She was alone, drifting without a home or family. She was on the run, wanted by the law just like him, and he'd believed the whole story.

They'd rarely parted company during their travels. Renée knew Jason would have observed even the tiniest details. She'd never tried to leave a sign or message for fear of being discovered. Though he'd never shown mistrust in her, she knew he'd survived his outlaw years by being suspicious of everything and everyone. She waited, probably thinking only patience would keep her alive.

Down in Texas, they'd lived in complete isolation. She couldn't get a message to Danton and Bonnie, so she'd pretended to fall in love. She'd said all the right things to make him fall in love with her too.

Then he realized something else. She had never made love to him, even after months of living together and talking about marriage. They hadn't even talked about it, and he'd simply thought she preferred to wait until they were married. She knew he wouldn't take advantage of her, or hurt her, or pressure her to do anything she didn't want to do. She knew that was his nature.

She'd used him. It was as simple as that. She'd put his heart out on the chopping block like a slab of beef to be carved up and roasted. She'd worked on his fantasies like the professional she was and had gotten him to ride the trail again so she'd get more opportunities to contact Danton and Bonnie. In Greenville, she'd finally gotten her chance.

Jason took the long way home. He rode slowly, wandering around the countryside aimlessly for three hours. Mostly, he just wanted to clear his mind and think things through. Partly, he wanted Bonnie Drake's posse, if they were nearby and following him, to think he had hit the trail without going back for his supplies. They wouldn't waste time at the cabin and would hit the trail fast to surround him. Then, he'd sneak back home behind them and get his trail supplies.

He dreaded riding around the last knobby hill into the valley that led to their cabin. He tried to stuff his hurt feelings away and prepare himself mentally to see Renée.

Or Shelley. Or whatever the hell her name is.

All the thinking in the world couldn't erase the pain that squeezed his heart like a steel vice and made him feel gutshot. He couldn't think away the manipulation and betrayal, nor his own hatred and love for the woman.

Jason didn't honestly know if he hurt more from being deceived or for loving her. For Christ's sake, he wanted to marry her and have children with her. It cut like a knife knowing she didn't want the same. It hurt even worse knowing she'd been pretending.

Now he understood the cleverness of Allan Pinkerton's controversial decision to hire women into his detective agency. No way any man could have gotten into his head like Renée had.

The complexity of the Pinkerton plans and the depth of Renée's knowledge of him boggled his mind. She knew almost everything a person could know about him. How many towns had she and her team visited collecting information about him? How many people had she and the others interviewed to produce a profile of how he thought, felt, and acted? With sickening admiration, he gained renewed respect for the Pinkertons.

Jason closed his eyes and took a deep breath as he approached the cabin. He knew exactly what he would do. He'd hide his pain deep inside, pack his belongings, and leave. There would be no confrontation or discussion, no threats or fights. Certainly, there would be no gunplay. He'd just leave her behind and pretend she never existed. He'd deal with the pain later, or try to anyway.

He opened his eyes, half expecting Bonnie's posse to charge at him across the open land. No one attacked, but from a quarter-mile away he saw a more disturbing sight. Debris littered the ground in front of the adobe cabin, and the door barely hung from its top hinge.

Jason pulled his Winchester and chambered a round.

CHAPTER 15

E RODE UP AND CAUTIOUSLY dismounted, but he could tell whoever had vandalized the cabin was long gone. He pushed the broken door aside and entered the cabin. The intruders had completely wrecked the inside and not for any other purpose than because they obviously enjoyed the destruction. They'd smashed the few items of furniture and tossed the debris out in front of the cabin. The wood stove was pushed over on its side, its exhaust pipe ripped loose from the ceiling. The window openings held no glass for the intruders to break, so they'd torn the shutters from the outside walls.

Jason walked out front and packed his Winchester away. He studied the tracks on the ground. Many wagons trampled the scrub grass yard. Two-wheeled carts and regular wagons had been used, heavily laden, judging by the depth of the ruts in the soft topsoil. He counted six sets of cart and wagon tracks. The tracks were a complete mess, but Jason counted maybe a dozen separate horse tracks, not counting the animals pulling the wagons.

Jason found more tracks farther away from the cabin. He saw deep impressions of high-heeled range boots forming a ring around a set of prints from hard- and soft-soled moccasins and bare feet. These men had prisoners.

He'd run across similar two-wheel cart tracks of Comancheros before, but after a few moments of inspection he realized this deed had been done by others. He knew Comancheros to be honest traders who traveled around the Southwest making their living buying and selling supplies, weapons, animals, or whatever else frontier settlers needed. They did not kidnap people or engage in illegal slave trade.

Jason realized slave traders had destroyed his cabin and made off with his woman. He'd heard about the raiders but never encountered them. They terrorized vulnerable settlers who lived far from town and were unable to adequately defend themselves, or those who had no law office or organized posse to protect them. They kidnapped anybody they could capture, then sold them into slavery south of the border or out west. They took payment in guns or gold.

These raiders had as much as a three-hour head start. Maybe only two. Jason went inside to take stock of his packs and weapons. Fortunately, he found them untouched by the raiders, safely hidden in the storage closet in the back room. He carried his packs out to his horse. He removed the saddle and brushed the animal down, then fed and watered it. Afterward, he saddled up and strapped his packs on. He checked all his weapons to make sure they were ready for use. He strapped on his double-gun holster and stuffed his two Colts into his belt. Then he stuck his boot in the stirrup, ready to mount up.

Then he hesitated.

What the hell am I doing? Getting ready to ride in pursuit of men who kidnapped the woman who betrayed me?

He removed his foot from the stirrup and slapped the animal on the rump. It moved off a few steps, then it stopped and began picking at the scrub grass. Jason sat down on the ground and leaned back against the adobe wall, near the broken door. He pulled the two uncomfortable guns from his belt and lay them on the ground beside him. Renée, the betrayer, would have killed him or arrested him within a day or two. Her capture could be the distraction he needed to escape if he left her for Bonnie and her posse to worry about. If Renée lived long enough, they'd find her and bring the raiders to justice. While they were busy, Jason could disappear on the open plains.

He removed his hat and looked up, squinting in the bright sunlight. There was only the big blue sky as far as he could see. That's what he loved most about the Southwest. The land was wide-open space under a big blue sky, and today there were only a few cotton-puff clouds scattered about the overhead canvas.

He put his hat back on and examined a particularly deep scuff mark on the tip of his right boot. He knew he should be riding out, but he couldn't find the energy to get up. He just sat there and absorbed the warmth of the sun. Then he dozed awhile.

The horse whinnied, and Jason awoke with a start. He looked up and saw a group of riders approaching, escorting a buggy around the hill. They were local folk, but still he didn't get up to welcome the riders.

Bonnie sat in the buggy, flanked by the doctor and Vince Parsons. Pain shaded her face, and she looked real pale.

She's got guts, Jason thought, *being that she was shot one hour and cutting my trail the next.* He respected her strength.

Frank Parsons and two other men rode alongside the buggy. Jason had seen them at nearby small ranches, but he didn't know their names.

"Howdy," Frank Parsons said in greeting. "She's got a Pinkerton badge, whatever that is." He shrugged. "Says she's a frontier detective."

"That she is," Jason answered. He eyed the shiny tin badge pinned to her coat. "Don't amount to much without her posse, though."

Bonnie ordered Vince Parsons to help her down from the buggy, then she dismissed the men and told them to wait for her out by the hill.

Jason added, "Take her gun with you, Mr. Parsons. Otherwise, I'm likely to shoot her again."

Bonnie wore pants and a brown plaid shirt under her coat. A holstered gun rested on her right hip. Parsons nodded to her, and she handed over the weapon. The men left, and she turned to face Jason. He stood and walked over to her.

They stared at each other wordlessly for a long time. He opened the flaps of her unbuttoned coat to see if she carried any hidden weapons. The left side of her shirt bulged over heavy bandages covering her bullet wound.

"What happened here?" she asked, nodding at the cabin door.

"Had some visitors while I was in town."

Bonnie glanced around at the tracks. "Comancheros?"

He shook his head. "Slave traders. I've heard they work this part of the country. Lots of open desert and not much law to answer to. They trade men, women, and children into slavery. All ages and colors."

Jason turned back to the cabin and retrieved his belt guns from the ground. He wiped dirt from them with a kerchief as he walked over to his horse. He stuck the guns in one of his packs within easy reach from the saddle. Then he mounted up and guided his horse in front of Bonnie. They stared at each other again, but he knew she saw the emotions in his eyes.

"You're just going to ride away? Leave her to die?"

"The way I see it, you've got to make a choice, Detective. I know you have a posse around here somewhere. Which do you want most—me dead or your sister alive?"

"My posse won't be here for three days, Jason."

"More time for me to get away," he said.

"She'll be dead by then."

"I suppose that's your problem now. You'd best get after her if you're able." He kicked his horse into a walk. "Can't be that hard for a professional like you to follow these tracks."

Jason stopped suddenly, reined up his horse. Something out of the ordinary caught his eye. He saw it in a passing glance—a mark that didn't fit with the other tracks in the grass and dirt.

"What is it?" Bonnie said.

Jason dismounted and squatted to inspect the oddity. He mumbled to himself and kept Bonnie waiting. She shouted at him.

"What!?"

She walked over unsteadily. Gasped in pain and clutched her left side as she knelt beside him. Jason studied a straight line, intentionally made among smudges that indicated someone had clawed around on the ground. Afterward, a horse had stomped on the line, but the ends of the line still existed. He followed the direction of the line and saw another mark a few inches away. The initials FW were carefully scratched in the dirt. The mark was hidden in the shadow of a tuft of scrub grass, made so that only an expert eye would find it.

"What does that mean?" she asked.

"FW is for Frenchwoman," he said. "Tell me, is Renée fully trained?"

Bonnie nodded. "Women detectives can shoot well and track, but we're especially trained in surveillance and information research."

"So she'll know how to leave signs. I'd suggest you get back to town and get your people here, pronto. You don't want to lose her trail. One good rain and these tracks will get washed away." He started to rise. Bonnie grabbed the sleeve of his coat.

"You know what these men will do to her?"

He nodded. "Rape, torture, slavery. You'd better not waste any time."

"You'd leave her to this fate because she was doing her job?"

"Her job?" He snatched his arm away.

Jason took a deep breath to control his outburst. He narrowed his eyes and glared at Bonnie. He trembled and clenched his fists to keep from venting his rage on the only target available to him.

Bonnie said gently, "You love her, don't you?"

"I did," he said angrily. "But she was just doing her goddamn job." He kicked his boot through the mark Renée had left for him. "Find your own damn sister." He started to turn away, then added, "If she really is your sister. You don't look much like her."

"We had different fathers. Mine died in a stampede. Mama remarried a few years later. Shelley...Renée...she's my half-sister."

He refused to listen to more lies. He looked around at the

empty land for a moment, then examined the ground between his boots.

"You're her only hope, Jason. She doesn't know you know the truth about her. She's out there somewhere, suffering, maybe dying. She's clinging to one thread of hope, that you love her and that you'll come for her. My men will be here too late. Only you have the skills to save her now. She believes you'll find her message and go after her." Bonnie sniffed away a tear. "And if you don't, she'll die out there somewhere, not knowing you've abandoned her, not knowing that no one is coming for her. You'd do that to her?"

Jason stared at the ground and stayed silent.

Bonnie took his hand in her own. "If you hadn't seen us in town, and you came back to find this." She swept her hand around. "What would you have done?"

Jason knew exactly what he would have done. He'd already be on Renée's trail. He would have done anything to get her back. Yet now he was going to turn his back on her. He was going to abandon the woman he loved because she had deceived him.

Bonnie continued. "Pretend you don't know the truth. Pretend you still love her as much as you did this morning."

"I don't..." His voice cracked. "I don't have to pretend."

He gazed into Bonnie's gentle eyes and saw Renée's eyes. He found comfort for a moment, then he snatched his hand away from hers. She was working him, playing on his feelings just like her sister had. Renée didn't love him. She cared not one whit about him. Neither did Bonnie. She just wanted him to rescue her sister. Then they'd arrest him.

"Call off the Pinkerton Agency."

Bonnie gasped. "You know I can't do that." Jason turned away and started to mount up.

"Jason," she called. "They've got a contract. I can't influence company policy."

He hoisted himself into the saddle.

"Wait!" Bonnie stammered for something to say. "I can lead

the posse up north, away from you. Give you a few weeks to escape to Mexico."

Jason shook his head. She might fool her posse for all of a day. Once they discovered her deception, she'd be replaced. The agency would just send someone else to take charge of the posse. He kicked his horse into a walk.

"Call 'em off. That's the price for your sister's life."

"She'll die if you don't go after her."

"I reckon she'll die then."

Jason nudged his horse to a trot. He passed the Parsonses without acknowledging them. With a full pack, he could survive for weeks without stopping anywhere for supplies. He'd head north, get lost up in the mountains. Maybe he'd visit Canada or double back and hide out in Mexico or Texas.

It don't matter, he thought. He'd figure out a destination somewhere along the trail.

He considered moving on to California but quickly discarded that thought. It would be just like Renée to have telegraphed Bonnie their previous destination in case the Pinkertons missed them in Greenville and lost the trail.

He tried to imagine a life without Renée. After a long while, he slowed his horse. Then he stopped. He turned in his saddle and looked back up the valley. He saw Bonnie and the others, but they were just tiny dots in the distance.

Between the two of them, the Drake sisters had jerked his strings any which way they'd wanted. He felt powerless against them because they'd studied him too well. They were professional masqueraders, and they'd appeared only as they wanted him to see them.

One thing he certainly knew Bonnie had not lied about. He was Renée's only hope to survive. Despite his wounded heart, he couldn't leave her or any other person, man or woman, lover or enemy, to suffer her fate. A week from now, abandoning her would hurt more than being deceived or arrested by her.

Jason turned his horse and rode slowly back to the cabin. He dismounted beside Bonnie Drake. "She left the initials FW because she knows a Frenchwoman would be worth a lot of money to her captors if she's unspoiled. That's her survival plan," he said.

Bonnie agreed. "You think as long as she can keep up the pretense, she'll be safe?"

"Keeping up pretenses shouldn't be a problem for her," Jason said harshly. Bonnie looked away as he tried to control his anger and his pain. After a moment, he continued. "They'll try to sell her to a very rich client. She's too expensive to let the dogs have her."

They stared at each other in silence. Bonnie leaned in for a quick hug that he did not return.

"I'll get your sister back," he said. "But if you follow me, I'll kill you and your posse. Of that, you should have no doubt."

CHAPTER 16

J ASON RODE FOR DAYS, STRAIGHT across northern Arizona. He passed through wide valleys, between hills, and into deep canyons carved between towering plateaus. He crossed riverbeds that saw water only during a passing thunderstorm. He followed the raiders' trail across Black Mesa Basin, an expanse of vast plateaus and valleys many miles wide.

The raiders never stopped for long. Jason could tell by their tracks that they frequently changed out the horse teams pulling the wagons. They kept pushing the animals hard, probably a long-standing plan aimed at outrunning all but a well-equipped pursuit that might be following. In their line of business, they had to know that someday someone would track them. Most pursuers would only be hastily organized posses of desperate family members. After a few days, they'd have to turn back to resupply or to try to enlist lawmen—if they could find any.

Jason passed many of the raiders' campsites and at each site he found Renée's marks easily. Five days out of Greenville, he came across a different camp. New riders had met the slave traders there. He saw signs of different horses, boots, and tobacco. He found such a jumble of tracks around the site, he couldn't decide if Renée continued north with the original carts or west with the new wagons.

Jason searched for over an hour for a distinctive sign from Renée, but he found nothing. That could only mean Renée didn't know which direction she would travel. Jason had to assume she would attempt to leave her mark after breaking camp, but it would have to be something that wouldn't be trampled by the horses and wagons.

Jason searched both departure paths for something she might have left behind. Maybe her hands had been tied. Perhaps she'd had to wait until the next stop. He made a choice, a wild-ass guess plucked out of thin air.

The tracks of the raiders turned north. Tracks of the new-comers' wagons led to the west. Jason guessed north. Three hours later, he found a camp where they'd stopped. He saw lots of prints but no sign from Renée.

After a methodical and painstaking search lasting nearly an hour, he stood frustrated and angry. She had to be with the westward group. Or maybe she was with this northbound group and was unable to leave a sign. Maybe she was hurt or uncon-scious, or worse.

Jason searched again. He spent another precious hour, but he had to be absolutely certain she'd left no sign. Wagon tracks, horses, pack mules, boots, and moccasins all mixed in together. He searched under every bush, every tuft of scrub grass, but still he found nothing.

Now he had a difficult decision to make. He'd been so close, maybe only a couple hours behind them. If he guessed wrong the first time and guessed wrong again, he'd lose nearly a whole day in the chase, and his gut told him she was running out of time if she'd been taken with the new group of riders.

Renée had to be with that other group. He mounted up, hesitated, looked off to the north, and felt a rare moment of self-doubt and indecision. If he missed something, she'd end up dead.

Jason kicked his horse into a run back to where the two trails split, then raced westward. An hour later, he found the place beside the trail where the fugitives had stopped to rest. He dismounted quickly, but then he stood still for a moment to stifle the overwhelming sense of panic he felt. He knew that if he stomped around in panic searching for evidence of her presence, he might carelessly step on that one mark she might have left.

So he stood absolutely still for five deep breaths. He'd succeeded in tracking and evading posses over the years, not by panicking but by maintaining complete control of his fear. Now Renée's life depended on his skill and control.

He scouted around methodically but quickly, starting with the area where the prisoners had gathered. Soon he found several FW marks. One of the reasons he loved her so much was because she was smart. She had left several marks in case one or two got trampled or erased.

Cursing himself again, Jason mounted up and hurried on his way. If he hadn't spent so much time on the other trail second-guessing himself, he'd be less than an hour behind them. Instead, he'd wasted half a day.

He pushed his horse steadily but not so fast that his horse would become winded. He rode straight through the day, stopping only briefly to rest and feed his horse. He ate sparse meals of dried beef jerky and biscuits in the saddle. By sunset, he had all but caught up with the raiders. He stopped to study still smoldering hand-rolled cigarettes they'd tossed carelessly along their trail. Foul-smelling chewing tobacco spit hadn't soaked into the dirt and dried yet. Half an hour more and he'd be on top of them.

A fiery sunset framed the ragged top of the rocky pass up ahead. The raiders had already set up camp there, he figured. They probably rode this trail so many times, they knew they'd arrive right before nightfall. Such a canyon would be easily defended too.

Jason rode into the darkness as close to the canyon entrance as he dared. Then, he led his horse off the path and ground-tied the animal. He grabbed two guns from his saddle pack and stuck those in his belt. He checked his Schofield holster guns and pulled his Winchester from its scabbard.

He handled the expensive weapon with almost loving tenderness. He'd won the superb rifle in a poker game and had come to appreciate its features. It was a new Model 1873, barely a couple of years out of the factory. It was worth a whopping hundred dollars, maybe more.

The 1873 Winchester, a rare version, featured an octagonal thirty-inch barrel. The color of its forged, case-hardened steel frame and lever was subdued instead of bright brass, like the Yellowboy and other older rifles. That made the weapon particularly useful for night work when he needed to avoid reflections from firelight or the moon. He checked its mechanism and found it fully loaded with thirteen shells. He chambered a round so he wouldn't risk being heard later, working the lever when he might need total surprise.

Jason stalked his enemy quickly and quietly. He located two useless lookouts up on the cliff tops, on either side of the narrow canyon. Instead of watching for intruders, they both concentrated their attention on the activity in the canyon below them. Sporadic gunshots erupted from the camp, punctuating screams of terror and raucous laughter.

He crept silently to the cliff edge beside a huge boulder and found the canyon shaped like a horseshoe. The south wall where Jason hid, angled steeply down toward the canyon floor, its slope covered with boulders and a few bushes.

A hundred feet across the canyon, the sheer north wall formed a natural curved amphitheater at the widest part of the horseshoe bend. To his surprise, the canyon floor rested less than thirty feet below the top of the cliff walls, much higher than the surrounding desert landscape outside the canyon.

A huge bonfire lit the center of the canyon floor, its flames casting eerie flickers of light and shadow on the cliff walls. A dozen armed men walked around laughing, drinking, and harassing their prisoners. Their vulgar sounds were magnified by the smooth walls of the amphitheater.

Jason found Renée huddled with the rest of the prisoners by the wagons. He saw three Black men, five or six White men, a couple of Indians, and about a dozen and a half women. They all cowered in fear under the threats and taunting of their captors.

More bullies, Jason thought, as the anger boiled inside him. He couldn't imagine living in such a state of terror as these people did. Never knowing when you'd be beaten or shot; powerless to stop these men from dragging your wife or daughter by the fire and raping her.

The raiders had picked the widest part of the pass to make their camp. Some of the men walked off behind the rocks around the far end to relieve themselves. Jason knew that's where he'd attack from. The lookouts on the east end of the pass couldn't reach him over there, but he knew there would be lookouts on the far side also. His biggest problem would be how to cover Renée's dash across the wide clearing to the boulders with snipers above or behind him.

Jason jumped into action. These men—these *animals*—were capable of anything, and Renée wasn't the only one in danger. He sensed he couldn't afford to waste another precious second.

He took a deep breath and began to make his way down through the boulders toward the west end of the pass he had spotted from above. He moved as fast and as carefully as he could, but it still took him a long ten minutes.

He peered into the darkness for the lookouts he knew were close by, but he saw no one above or behind him. He peeked over a rock to scout the area for guards and strategies, but his attention was immediately drawn toward a scream near the bonfire. Two women were being dragged away from the others and toward the fire.

One of the women was Renée.

CHAPTER 17

T HE TWO GUARDS THREW THE women to the ground and tore at their coats. Jason immediately brought up his Winchester and took aim at the man hovering over Renée. A gunshot echoed in the night and dirt exploded at the feet of Renée's attacker. A short, wiry man approached Renée and stuck his gun to her attacker's head. He spoke a few words. The attacker nodded furiously and backed away.

The small man carried an air of undisputed authority about him. He helped Renée to her feet and led her back to the rest of the hostages. Then the leader shouted more commands around the suddenly still camp. Jason couldn't hear the words over the fierce crackle of the huge bonfire, but he understood the message. No one would harm the Frenchwoman.

The two would-be rapists dragged the Indian woman by her arms toward the west end of the horseshoe curve, out of sight of the rest of the camp. She kicked and screamed in vain. They were headed where Jason would be in a few minutes. Hopefully, he'd find a way to take advantage of them when they were most distracted.

As Jason crept through the boulders, intent on intercepting the men, he heard a coyote yelp close by but slightly higher in the rocks. He froze. Such an animal would never hunt or scavenge close to humans, especially not at night. He waited for the next sound, unsure whether the call was a coordinated communication or a warning. Almost immediately, he heard an unseen lookout perched on the boulder right above him turn toward the animal sound. The man's boots crunched against rock as the man pivoted.

Jason knew had he taken one more step, he'd have been spotted and shot in the back. Somewhere in the darkness nearby he had an ally, someone on the same mission as he was. He waited for his cue to take action. He heard it in the swish of an arrow, a thump and a gasp from above. Jason moved quickly, knowing instinctively what to do.

He dropped his Winchester and scrambled up onto the boulder. He saw the feathered shaft sticking out of the shocked man's chest, the arrowhead protruding from his back. He caught the man's falling rifle with one hand and grabbed him by the suspenders with his other. Quickly, he yanked the man with him as he jumped off the boulder and was rewarded with a muted crack of neck bones as the man fell headfirst to the ground.

Jason ducked as he heard the would-be rapists behind him. He glanced over his shoulder. He saw one of the men throw the Indian woman to the ground by the collar of her coat. She struggled heroically, but the man hit her hard in the jaw. Dazed, she groaned, unable to fight off her attacker. The man pulled her coat off, turned her onto her back, and then yanked her deerskin dress up.

Unfortunately, Jason's ally was screened from the woman's attackers by a huge boulder, so he waited until the attacker rose slightly to pull down his pants. When he did so, his body hid Jason's approach from the second man. In three quick running steps, Jason flashed past the first man. He slammed the stock of the lookout's rifle into the surprised face of the second. It was too dark in the shadows to see the damage he had inflicted, but he could tell he'd hit the man hard enough to kill him.

The first man wasted precious seconds pulling his pants back up, just as Jason knew he would. The man opened his mouth to shout a warning and Jason pivoted, launching a front kick to his face. He caught him in the mouth with his boot heel and snapped his head back, but the man was big and strong—

more than 200 pounds. He recovered quickly and swung to his left to face the threat.

Not wanting to risk a rifle shot that would alert the camp, Jason dropped his weapon. He darted behind the dazed attacker and used the man's own momentum to wrestle him to his hands and knees, just as he would have thrown down a calf for branding. He covered the man's mouth with his left hand and ripped his carving knife from a belt sheath with his right. He worked it into the man's throat like he would cut a tough piece of rawhide.

Then he made a mistake and all hope of a quick and quiet kill vanished in an instant of clumsiness.

He'd never cut a man's throat before. He thought the sharp, six-inch blade would easily accomplish the deed. He figured he could simply hold the man still until he suffocated or bled to death. Instead, Jason found himself struggling to cut through hard gristle and muscle. His victim thrashed about as Jason ripped and tore the knife through his throat. Blood splattered everywhere. The warm, slick wetness spilled over the man's face, over the Indian woman's face and clothes, and over Jason's hands. He struggled to hold the man, but his bloody hands kept slipping.

A raging, wounded animal, the attacker clawed at him, refusing to die. Jason had to let him go, and the man's wail of pain and terror exploded into the night. He turned toward Jason and charged—murder in his eyes.

The man's neck spurted blood in pulses from his severed veins and arteries. Jason fell to the ground as he stumbled away from the wild man. Lying on his rump, he pulled a gun from his belt and shot him in the head.

Then everything seemed to happen at once. Camp sounds echoed with individual clarity in Jason's mind. Surprise lost, he could only think of saving Renée. He heard the metallic snap of a rifle lever up on the ridge, across the clearing. Then the twang of a bow pierced the air. An arrow whistled into the distance. Jason glanced up and, though he couldn't see the arrow in the dark, he realized it struck the lookout with enough force to knock him back off his feet. The man fell to the canyon floor, screaming.

Jason cursed at his lost advantage. He grabbed the Indian woman, threw her across his shoulder, and carried her higher up into the boulders. There he dumped her unceremoniously to the ground and thrust his belt gun into her hands. He turned and ran back down to search for Renée. He looked for the Winchester or the other rifle, knowing they were lying around nearby, but had no time to find either one as he ran toward the camp.

Jason began to feel the prickly fingers of panic squeeze his gut. He crouched behind a boulder at the edge of the clearing. Raiders ran everywhere, guns blazing. The wiry leader shouted, and this time Jason heard him clearly over the crackling flames.

"Load up the prisoners or shoot them!"

Some of the raiders shepherded prisoners into the wagons. Others hitched up the horses. Still others cut down escaping prisoners with deadly accurate gunfire.

Jason saw Renée running across the clearing, helping an older woman. Renée headed toward the boulders on Jason's side of the pass. He pulled his remaining belt gun but held his fire, not wanting to draw attention to her. Briefly moving from behind his boulder, he waved at her so she could see him.

Renée held onto the woman prisoner by one arm and the back of her coat, practically dragging the woman along with her. Finally, she saw Jason. They made eye contact, and she changed her direction, heading straight for him.

Jason willed her to hurry, but she made slow progress. Without the other woman, she would have been safe already in his arms. He saw desperation in her eyes. He saw determination and relief—along with love that must be false.

A gunshot echoed and dirt puffed beside Renée. Jason turned toward the threat and found two men aiming. He fired twice and hit both men. When he turned back to Renée, he saw her glancing to her left, eyes widening in horror. Two horses thundered into view too late for Jason to react.

The lead rider aimed at Renée, too close to miss. Jason heard the zip of an arrow even as the rider pulled his trigger. The arrow hit the man in the side of his chest, and his body was ripped from the saddle. Jason fired twice at the second rider just as the first tumbled to a stop in Renée's path. She helped the woman prisoner over the dead body, nearly tripping on the arrow shaft protruding from the man's side.

Jason had no choice but to wait. Just a few more steps and she'd be safe. Ten paces. Time moved painfully slow as he watched. Every step took an eternity.

Five paces. Four.

The woman stumbled, nearly dragging Renée down, but somehow Renée kept them both on their feet. Jason started forward to help them.

Three paces.

As he stepped into the clearing, he dropped his gun and reached out for the woman he loved.

Two paces.

Then he saw movement in the darkness behind Renée.

One pace.

One of the men he'd shot still lived and was aiming at the women from a prone position. In half a heartbeat, Jason grabbed for his right holster. There was no time to think or aim. He had no time for anything but instinct. All the God-given talent and all the years of practice meant nothing now except for a single reflex action—his fastest quick-draw ever. He had one chance to keep Renée alive, whether she loved him or not.

Renée-Simone or Renée Shelley or Shelley Drake or whatever name she used—was the woman who would turn him over to the Pinkerton Agency, but she was still the woman he loved with all his heart.

In a flash of desperation he drew, aimed, and shot all in one motion, but he was too late. His bullet ripped open the shooter's head a split second after the man fired.

Both women pitched forward into the dirt at Jason's feet.

CHAPTER 18

J ASON FELL ATOP THE WOMEN to keep them from moving. He pretended to be dead to stay alive. The woman prisoner flinched at every sound, struggling to get free, but Jason held her down. He pleaded with her to remain silent and still. Renée lay still beneath him, barely breathing. He fingered the bullet hole in her coat. The shot had hit her high in the back.

Face down, he heard prisoners screaming across the camp. Raiders shouted and cussed and fired their guns. Horses raced out of the canyon pulling wagons and carts on creaking wheels. The last sounds of the raiders' departure echoed off the smooth rock walls of the amphitheater, and finally the flames of the bonfire made the only sounds.

Jason crawled off the women and rolled Renée over. He pulled her into his lap. She looked up at him, smiled, and tried to speak. He placed a finger against her lips and spoke to her of his undying love and of their new home in northern California and of all the children they'd have.

He rocked her gently and hugged her, then kissed her. He felt her last breath on his lips and watched her beautiful brown eyes close forever. He held her still body for a long while.

When finally Jason looked up, he realized the woman Renée had given her life for was squatting next to him. She placed her hand on his shoulder, and he turned as she spoke.

"Are you Jason Peares? The outlaw?"

He nodded. "I am."

"She said you'd come for her."

"What's your name, ma'am?"

"Constance Morgan."

He studied her for a moment. She looked about fifty or fifty-five and had dark eyes with graying hair. Heavyset, she had a round face with leathery skin. He figured she was probably a farmer, a woman who shared the hard work of earning a living beside her man.

"Miss Morgan, you're alive because of her. I want to make sure you're real clear about that."

She nodded. "If not for her, I'd have died long before today." She paused. "She loved you deeply."

Jason turned away from Constance Morgan and considered her words. Why would the Pinkerton detective tell a fellow hostage that fabrication? Then he recalled the tenderness in Renée's eyes in her last moments of life. Maybe some kind of love had grown between them during their months on the run, despite her task of capturing him. He closed his eyes and wiped tears from his cheeks. Clearly, whatever they'd had wasn't enough to prevent her from doing her job by reporting their location to her partners.

He took a deep breath and tried to separate what he knew from what he hoped was true. There had to have been love between them. It couldn't all have been a lie. But when he tried to recollect the words whispered by campfires, the promises spoken, the tender hugs shared, he found it was all a hazy cloud. It was as if the past few months had been ripped from his memory.

Finally, he said, "No, Miss Morgan, she didn't love me. But she did a damn good job of pretending." That was the only conclusion that made sense to him.

He reloaded his Schofield with shells from his gun belt and stuck it back in its holster pocket. Then he retrieved his Colt from beside the boulder at the edge of the clearing. He reloaded it and tucked the weapon in the front of his pants. He stood and scanned the steep hill above him for his invisible ally, but he saw no one.

Sleep eluded Jason the entire night, but Constance Morgan slept next to him curled up almost in a ball. It was probably her first decent sleep in weeks. He couldn't begin to imagine the fear and horror she and the others had experienced during their captivity. Several times during the night she awoke with a start. He patted her shoulder through her heavy coat and told her repeatedly she was safe and that he wouldn't let anything happen to her.

The sky lightened long before daylight and cast away the deep shadows of the canyon. During the early hours, his silent ally had shown himself. The warrior and the woman Jason had saved busied themselves around the camp. When Miss Morgan finally awoke around noon, she and Jason joined the two Indians at the smoldering bonfire for a brief meal of venison and bread.

Afterward, the men dragged the dead bodies onto the pile of smoking wood, then stoked up the flames again. Constance Morgan said some words for the souls of the dead prisoners and raiders despite Jason's suggestion not to pray for her captors.

Earlier in the morning, the Indian woman had retrieved Jason's horse and the warrior's ponies and pack mules. He tried to thank the Indians for their help, but they couldn't find a common language. Through the exchange of sign and gesture, Jason learned the two were mates. The woman carried the warrior's unborn child. He knew saving the man's wife had earned him a lifelong friend.

He studied them as they conferred in their unfamiliar language. She had discarded her torn garments and now wore another deerskin dress, tight-fitting, with long sleeves and a high neckline. She also wore deerskin leggings and had tied back her long black hair.

The warrior stood three inches taller than Jason. His broad shoulders tapered to a narrow waist. He wore a sleeveless deerskin shirt and leggings—plain and simple without distinctive markings or decorations. The strong, sinewy muscles of his arms rippled when he moved. The leather of his hard-soled moccasins reached halfway up his calves. The man had a narrow, hard face with high cheekbones and sharp features. He gazed at Jason through dark emotionless eyes. With skin several shades darker than Jason's, he looked tanned by many years in the southwestern sun. He wore his black hair in two loose braids hanging over his shoulders. Jason thought warriors always wore war paint in battle, but this one did not.

While the warrior and his woman conversed, Jason searched for and retrieved his Winchester and carving knife. He cleaned both and slid the rifle into its scabbard. After that, he pulled his rain slicker from his pack and wrapped Renée's body tightly, then lifted her across the saddle.

The warrior spoke. In his outstretched palm, he held a long knife enclosed in an intricately designed sheath. Jason took the knife and watched while the warrior told his story with pictures in the dirt. If he could believe the heroic tale, the warrior had killed the head bull of a herd of buffalo with only a single broken arrow for a weapon. Then he'd carved the blade Jason held from the leg bone of that big buffalo.

Jason removed the weapon from its sheath and examined it. The knife featured a one-piece blade and handle, blue-gray in color. It was perfectly balanced where the handle and blade met. He held the ten-inch blade in front of his face and studied its razor-sharp edges. If he'd had that knife last night, he could have sliced the attacker's neck like soft lard. He would have done the deed quietly, and Renée would still be alive.

Jason slid the knife back into its sheath. He tied the sheath to his calf and made sure the leather loop kept the weapon in place. He'd put the knife to excellent use when he found the men who had stolen Renée from him. Before he could finish that business, he had to tell Bonnie Drake he couldn't save her sister.

Without announcement, Jason grabbed the reins and led his horse out of the canyon. He made no attempt to explain where he headed, nor did he invite the others to accompany him. Instinct told him the warrior would follow him to the shores of both oceans to help him find Renée's killers. He suspected the man saw the determination in his eyes and knew his destination and what he would do when he got there.

Before he could attend to the raiders, he had to deal with the Pinkerton detectives.

CHAPTER 19

J ASON AND THE WARRIOR WALKED side by side along the trail that traversed the plateau. Constance Morgan and the warrior's mate rode the ponies. They followed a few paces back, leading the pack mules. They made slow progress, only ten or fifteen miles a day. In fact, Jason felt no need to hurry. He knew Bonnie Drake and her posse would be along shortly.

Through the long hours together, neither Jason nor his new friend attempted conversation. For his part, Jason felt no desire to converse. He suspected the warrior had even less need to talk. Near noon of the third day, the warrior spoke a single word and pointed ahead. Jason stared at the distant figures. He pulled his gun belt from his pack and strapped it on. Then he pulled the two Colts from his pack and stuck them in his belt.

Jason walked around his horse and prepared his Spencer, single-shot long rifle. Next he pulled his Winchester and chambered a round. He turned to motion the women to fall back, but they had already turned away. They rode a quarter-mile away and waited.

The warrior had disappeared while Jason unpacked his guns. One moment he walked alongside Jason, the next he'd become part of the landscape. Jason scanned the open land but saw only scrub grass and an occasional bush.

During his years in the cattle and ranch business, Jason had spent time trading and hunting with many Indian tribes, but he'd never traveled with a warrior. He felt a kindred spirit with this particular man, who also seemed to be a loner by choice despite having a family. He was a man of few words and fewer friends, as far as Jason could tell. He felt an intuitive trust of the man, deeper than any bond he'd felt before.

Four years ago, he'd trusted his best friend Sam. Then Sam had tried to turn him in for the bounty. The boy died in a reckless gunfight with a posse, taking one of Jason's bullets in the chest. Jason had trusted Renée because he loved her and thought she loved him. Now she was dead too.

The warrior was different. The kinship Jason felt with the man was deeper than instinct and honor. It was more like a feeling of competition. They hardly knew each other, and each possessed vastly different skills. Yet he knew in his soul the man felt the same competition. Each wondered which of them was better at their particular business.

Jason scanned the landscape again and still saw no sign of the warrior. With satisfaction, he nodded to himself. Bonnie Drake and her posse had a rude surprise coming if they decided to make a mess of things.

The detectives stopped half a mile away. Jason watched as Bonnie rode forward alone to meet him. She pulled up short and said nothing for a long moment. Then she dismounted and walked over to his horse. She looked at the bundle for a moment, then pulled back the slicker and hugged Renée's body. Bonnie sobbed quietly for a few minutes.

Jason offered her the comfort of a hand on her shoulder.

Finally, she faced him and wiped her eyes with her kerchief. "What happened?"

Jason looked away. "I...made a mistake." His voice cracked. "I couldn't save her. She died in my arms."

"Did you tell her you know the truth?"

He lowered his head. "I told her I loved her. That was the truth."

"Thank you," Bonnie said. She paused a moment, looking beyond Jason's horse. "Who are they?"

"Prisoners. Turns out both are alive because of my blunder.

One on the left is alive because of Renée. The other is the mate of a friend."

"A friend?"

He nodded. "He's around."

Bonnie Drake scanned the area for a moment, then looked him in the eye. "Don't make this difficult, Jason. I'm arresting you."

"You can arrest me after I see to the men who killed Renée." Those men had to pay for their crime against the woman he loved. Whether or not Renée felt the same love was irrelevant. That fact was suddenly very clear in his mind. No one and nothing would stand between Jason and the men who'd killed Renée.

"That's not acceptable."

"It'll have to be unless you and your men are ready to die." He saw Bonnie considering the situation. "You know weapons, right?" he added.

She nodded.

"Look at my Spencer." As Bonnie studied the weapon, he said, "It's a specially modified, single-shot, long rifle with a forty-four-inch barrel and a four-power scope."

"It's a beautiful piece."

"I picked it up in California three years ago, on the run from Marshal Gallagher and his posse."

She nodded. "We interviewed them last year."

"That Spencer fires .50-caliber rounds. I can take a man out nearly a mile away and your men are much closer than that." He paused while she considered her predicament.

"Ever see what a .50-caliber shell does to a man? It's real messy, Bonnie. It'll go right through a man and whoever is standing in front or behind. Hell of a way to die. And my warrior friend is somewhere out there with a bow or a rifle or both. Your men won't have a chance."

He watched Bonnie as she scanned the land around them again. He watched her eyes and saw Renée's eyes again. They were light brown, deep and piercing, and highly intelligent. Today, she looked a lot younger and much prettier than he'd thought when she kissed him in the saloon in Salina. Maybe only ten years his senior. Thirty-five, he guessed. Back then, she'd powdered herself up to fit her disguise. Now her plain features gave her a wise and weathered frontier look, and she was not at all unattractive.

Finally, she spoke. "What are you proposing?"

"Enough good people have died already. Now it's time for the bad ones to die. Go back and see to your sister and give me time to find the men who killed her. Take Miss Morgan with you." Jason prayed she would accept his offer. He didn't want to be responsible for killing both the Drake sisters.

Bonnie looked toward her men in the distance and shook her head. "The company would never agree to that. The burial will take a week. You could be halfway to Canada. Or in Mexico."

A distant part of him wondered where Bonnie would bury her sister. He really had no idea of where Renée had called home. Everything he knew about her was a lie. "Only if that's where Renée's killers are headed." Jason turned and waved at Constance Morgan, then waited while the woman rode her pony up beside him. "Miss Morgan, this is Bonnie Drake of the Pinkerton National Detective Agency. She'll see that you get home safe."

While Bonnie and Constance exchanged greetings, Jason slid his Winchester into its scabbard. He gently moved Renée's body to Bonnie's horse. He laid his forehead against the body for a moment, then turned to face Bonnie.

"Isn't this what you really want?" Jason said. She didn't answer. "I can do what your agency can't do. What they won't allow you to do."

"We'll be issuing warrants for their capture. The company will want to bring these criminals to justice."

"Save your paper and ink, Bonnie," Jason said quietly. "I'm not interested in delivering arrest warrants or justice. I'll find them and I'll kill them, but I need time."

She stared at him again. Finally, she relented. "One week, Jason. Then I'm back on your trail."

Jason nodded and mounted up.

"Mr. Peares," Constance Morgan said. "Hunting and killing those men won't bring Shelley back."

He nudged his horse close to her and stared at her a few seconds, but she didn't look away. "I'll have that pony now, Miss Morgan."

She dismounted. "I'm sure you know vengeance is for the Lord to deliver," she said, handing Jason the rawhide reins.

"God didn't save your life, Miss Morgan. Shelley Drake did. And today, vengeance is mine because her killers have to pay."

"She talked a lot about you and she loved you, whether you believe that or not. I think she'd rather you ride off to save people than to kill."

Jason looked down at her as she spoke, his piercing brown eyes devoid of emotion.

Constance Morgan continued speaking. "Mr. Peares, those men are holding a lot of prisoners that need saving."

"I'm not interested in saving anyone," Jason said, reining his horse around.

Constance called after him. "From everything Shelley told me about you, I don't believe you're a murderer."

Jason stopped his horse and turned in his saddle. "I'm not," he said quietly. "Not yet. But believe me, Miss Morgan, when I find her killers, I will be." He looked from Constance Morgan to Bonnie Drake, then back. "Of that you should have no doubt."

CHAPTER 20

T HE TRACKS OF THE RAIDERS led west, then up into high pine country and across a mountain range. Jason and the warrior followed the tracks back down into the expanse of desert, then over the mesas. They kept up a steady pace, passing messy campsites without stopping and closing the distance on the enemy. After twelve days in pursuit, he knew they'd catch the raiders the next day.

Jason figured the raiders would eventually have to turn south if they were headed to Mexico, or north to find a way across the big canyon if they were headed to California. Instead, he caught up with them in a place called Hell-Town, in the shadow of the towering third mesa.

Out of the barren stretch of desert, devoid of everything except scrub brush, a scattering of clapboard shacks rose along the bank of a dried-up creek. A large, well-built saloon added a semblance of class to the town that otherwise had absolutely no redeeming qualities.

Jason circled around the town and rode in from the northwest. He headed straight for the saloon. He passed a ragged corral that held the wagons and carts, as well as the horses used to pull them. Four men guarded the animals and equipment. They regarded him with what he could only guess was malevolent curiosity as he rode by, but he ignored them. He simply acted as if he belonged in town.

The town was deserted, except for the saloon and a shack

he guessed to be the prisoners' bunkhouse. He ignored the eyes watching him from the windows of the shack, pleading silently to him for help. He saw only a single guard at the prisoners' shack with good reason. Hell-Town sat a hundred miles from nowhere. The prisoners might escape, but they wouldn't get far without food, water, or horses.

As he dismounted, laughter erupted from the saloon, punctuated by a woman's scream that was cut short by a hard slap. More laughter followed. Jason tied up to the rickety hitching post. There was no boardwalk, so he coughed loudly to announce his presence before entering the saloon. Then he pushed casually through the door of the saloon. He paused, facing nearly two dozen guns.

Jason let the door swing closed behind him and was immediately hit by a cacophony of rancid smells as he scanned the room of hostile faces. He studied the men, filthy denizens who hadn't shaved or bathed for weeks. They stank of foul breath, body odor, and bad whiskey. Most of the men were dressed appropriately to survive the harsh desert weather. Some wore ponchos over their shirts and pants. Others wore long bag breeches extending to their knees, with long stockings and hard-soled moccasins. A couple of the men gazed at Jason under pointed sombreros. Three had their faces painted up like they were on the warpath. Some of the men without hats wore headbands over their long, unruly hair. Still others simply wore their mop of hair braided over their shoulders. The mix of clothing and accoutrements was an odd sight that Jason didn't often encounter from frontier outlaws.

All the men looked downright mean. They all had dirty faces with nappy beards, tangled mustaches, and unshaven necks. Those who scowled at him had rotting teeth. Some of the men pointed one or two pistols at him. Others held long-barrel guns or sawed-off shotguns, perfect weapons for close-quarters, scrappy fighting.

Jason knew the honest Comanchero trade business had been all but wiped out in the early seventies. Originally, they were known as travelers who traded mostly with the Comanche Indians of west Texas, but they had suffered an increasingly bad reputation over the last twenty years. It was undeserved in Jason's opinion, mostly caused by a few notorious villains who emulated the Comancheros' mode of travel—the two-wheel cart—and chose to work outside the law.

Because of the terrible deeds of relatively few renegade traders, most states had outlawed the desert trade practice, and lawmen hunted down the Comancheros like animals. A few illegal bands of outlaws still wandered the deserts and were usually composed of only the hardest and most unscrupulous of the traders. They traveled with their carts and spent their time trading guns, stolen cattle, and slaves of all races to whoever would pay.

Jason's gaze settled finally on the leader. He was the small wiry man he'd seen in the horseshoe canyon. He nodded to the man with a single up-down movement of his head. A hint of a smile creased the corner of his mouth—the kind of sinister sneer that put outlaws in league with each other. It was a look that bespoke more credentials than any amount of words could. It was the look that said, "I'm not your friend, but I'm not your enemy."

"You suppose I could get a drink in here?" he said to the leader.

"I sure hope you aren't the law," the man answered in heavily accented English.

"Sir, I've been accused of being many things, but no one has ever called me a lawman." Jason smiled more openly. "Besides, even if I was, I certainly wouldn't confess to being as such, not with all that hardware pointed my way."

The small man smiled in return. He showed two gaps in his ragged line of yellow and brown teeth. His brown, ruddy complexion gave him a rugged, sinister look. Beady, dark eyes were sunk deep in his thin face under smooth black eyebrows. His hawklike nose divided his face into two uneven halves.

The man stood and walked over to Jason. Immaculate shoulder-length, black hair and a perfectly trimmed mustache and goatee gave him an air of shrewdness and intelligence.

"And who might you be, Señor?"

The man's gaze drifted down to Jason's two belt guns, then farther down to his low-slung double-gun holster.

"Name's Jason Peares." He paused as a wave of gasps and murmurs rippled through the raiders. Like nearly everyone else across the western frontier, these men knew of his reputation. "I've got some angry Pinkerton detectives on my trail. I'd be grateful if you send 'em off to the south when they get here, 'cause I'm headin' north."

"I'm Miguel Cordova," the leader said, putting his guns away. His men did the same. "Pinkerton detectives, eh? How'd you manage to get on the wrong side of the Pinkerton Agency?"

Jason decided to stick to the truth. There was less chance of getting caught in a lie that way.

"I had a conversation with six of them who caught up with me over in Kansas. Unfortunately, the discussion involved gunplay, and now their associates are looking to even the score. They've been hassling me for a while."

Cordova wore a look of ridicule on his face. "Am I to believe you dispatched six men in a single gunfight? Six Pinkerton men?"

Jason shook his head. "Only five. The sixth froze up and didn't draw. The next time I saw him, though, he wasn't as smart. Now there's six more of them from the original dozen, but they're a tad angry with me."

"Just a tad?" Cordova nodded and motioned Jason to the bar. "Well, when they get here, maybe we'll take care of the rest of them for you."

"I'm obliged, Mr. Cordova," Jason said. "But I wouldn't want you and your boys to go and get in any trouble with the law."

Cordova and his men burst into laughter.

Jason briefly eyed three shirtless men standing at the back of the room. They weren't laughing with the rest of Cordova's men. They were prisoners, Jason knew instantly. Two looked fairly young. One was White and the other was Black. The third man was an elder native man, bent over a bit at the waist, bones encased in a sack of skin. His frazzled, white hair draped over his sagging shoulders.

Jason looked down at the much shorter Miguel Cordova and then casually leaned against the bar. It was a long wood plank nailed to upturned wine barrels stacked three high. Cordova gestured to the bartender, a big ugly man with missing teeth and a fringe of long brown hair below the bald dome of his head. He stood behind his female captive. Dried blood crusted over the right side of her nose and mouth. Her right eye was bruised deep purple and swollen almost shut.

The barkeep ordered the woman to pour two whiskeys. When she didn't move fast enough, he slapped her upside the head so hard she nearly fell under the bar. She grabbed the plank to catch herself and struggled unsuccessfully to keep the contents of the bottle from spilling. The bartender hit her again, and the men behind Jason erupted again in laughter.

When she scrambled to her feet, Jason saw inside her torn shirt. She saw him looking at the bruises on her naked breasts, then closed her shirt with one hand. As she poured, she gazed at him behind a mop of unruly brown hair that now hid most of her face. It was a look of pure desperation that implored mercy or rescue.

The woman had been badly beaten and tortured or probably worse. Jason knew he stood among the kind of men who would do such deeds and feel no remorse. In every lawless town he'd ever passed through, men like these treated the weak mercilessly. The woman wouldn't survive the day. Still, Jason looked away from her and put on an expression that said he didn't care.

Constance Morgan's words came to mind.

Those men are holding a lot of prisoners that need saving.

He tried to tell himself he didn't care about these people. The woman trying to serve him a drink certainly needed his help, but he couldn't allow himself to be distracted from his purpose.

Renée's killers had to die. Nothing could interfere with that. He realized Cordova was speaking.

"You're just in time for the entertainment, Señor," Cordova said, jerking his head toward the three prisoners. "We shall see which of these men most wants to live." He nodded to one of his men.

"Pick up those axes! Now!" the man said, pointing a gun at them. "Last man standing lives. If you don't fight, you die."

The three men faced each other. The old man could hardly lift his axe. Jason knew he wouldn't last a second. As the woman filled the second dirty glass, the mouth of the bottle jingled against the rim of the glass. Jason saw her hand trembling as she pushed the glass toward him.

"Please help me," she whispered. "I'll do anything."

The barkeep cursed and hit her upside the head again, but this time she kept her balance.

She pleaded, "Anything."

She grabbed Jason's hand as he reached for his glass. He twisted his hand away and looked in her eyes. He saw defeat there. She would die today, and she knew it.

"Sorry, Miss," he said. "I didn't come here to get involved in your problems."

It was the same thing he'd told Renée months ago. He didn't abide by those words back then, and he knew he wouldn't today either. He turned away from the bar and raised his glass to Cordova in salute. The man raised his in return.

"To survival," Cordova proclaimed loudly. He nodded toward the back of the room where the Black man and the White man circled each other, axes waving. All the occupants of the saloon had turned their attention to the fighters.

"To the Frenchwoman," Jason said loudly. Cordova's eyes widened in surprise just before Jason slammed his whiskey glass into his face.

Cordova careened off the bar as his outlaws turned in surprise. The prisoners leaped forward, axes swinging, and caught two of the raiders in the back of their skulls.

Jason pulled his holster guns and started shooting before Cordova's unconscious body hit the stained floor. The raiders recovered quickly from their surprise, though. They threw their ponchos aside and pulled back their untucked shirts to get to their guns.

They pushed and shoved each other, panicked in the confines of the room, while Jason chose his targets quickly and carefully. Men quick to bring up their shotguns, very dangerous weapons in a barroom brawl, died first.

Jason's weapon of first choice, the Schofield pistol, had tremendous stopping power. A definite man-stopper, the .45-caliber fired a big slug from a cartridge packed with a powerful charge of powder. At close range, one scoring shot usually took down even the strongest man, but not like the dime novels he'd read where men dropped dead instantly from a single bullet. A .45 tore you up inside and ripped huge chunks of your body apart. It tossed you around with its tremendous impact force, and when you finally hit the ground, it paralyzed you with shock. The weapon let you think upon your sins for the few minutes it took you to die.

Jason fired repeatedly. His bullets ripped into the chests of his targets, scrambling vital organs into mush. The force of his shots slammed men against the walls and tossed them over tables. His slugs severed limbs and exploded chest cavities and spines as they tore through the raiders' bodies. Blood splattered everywhere. Screams of agony echoed over the explosions of Jason's rapid gunfire. Then he twirled his empty guns back to his holsters and pulled his belt guns and continued firing.

The men who finally got to their guns fired wildly. Some tried to escape, running for the door, but Jason's gunfire cut them down in midstride. Within a few seconds, he had no more targets. All of Cordova's men lay dead or dying, either from Jason's guns or from axe wounds.

About to tuck away his last belt gun, Jason heard a metallic sound behind him—a knife blade sliding from its sheath. He turned and pointed his gun at the barkeep's head.

"I'll cut her throat," the man said. "I swear it."

Jason merely chuckled and tucked his gun away. "I thought you were aimin' to use that pig sticker on me."

He turned and called over to the prisoners. "Grab up some guns and go see to the men guarding the horses." As they followed his command, Jason turned his attention back to the bartender.

"What you do with the woman is your business. I came for Mr. Cordova." Jason glanced down at the unconscious man. "But I wouldn't mind another drink, though."

The barkeep nodded warily, his gaze shifting between Jason and the armed prisoners. He put his knife away and shook the woman as if to reinforce the command. She stared at Jason in disbelief, and he knew if she'd had any anger left in her she'd be cussing him all the way back to the beginning of his family line. Instead, she nodded and flinched when the bartender raised his hand as if to hit her again. She obediently reached for the whiskey bottle and began pouring another glass.

At the same time, Jason kicked his right leg up, unlatched the leg sheath, and pulled out the buffalo bone knife. The barkeep must have caught a glimpse of his movement because he dodged his head away just as Jason plunged the ten-inch blade toward his eye.

He missed his target and instead the blade opened a pink gash along the side of the man's dirty skull. The woman didn't miss, though. She swung the whiskey bottle backhanded and bounced the nearly full bottle off the man's face. He staggered back, dazed. Before Jason could get a gun up for a clear shot, the woman hit him again three more times. Then the bottle finally shattered, spilling liquid over his head.

She screamed like a wild woman and broke everything she could find over his head until he finally fell to the floor. Next, she pulled the plank and wine barrel bar over on top of him. She kicked him until she had no strength left to lift her leg.

Jason watched her, but he didn't interfere. Cordova stirred, but Jason kicked him in the head to put him back to sleep. He watched the woman stalk around like a cat, searching for something else to hit the bartender with. She crossed the room and grabbed a gun from one of the dead raiders. She emptied it into the man, threw the weapon at his dead body, found a shotgun, and did the same thing again.

Jason grabbed her as she searched for another gun. She screamed and turned on him, swinging a fist that missed. He pulled her close and held her tight, wincing as she clung to him and clawed his back and shoulders, and she wept. Nearly spent, her trembles subsided quickly. After a long time, she moved away and pulled her shirt together while Jason turned his attention to Cordova. As the man began to regain his senses a second time, Jason hauled him up by the back of his collar. He heaved him through the door into the middle of the hostile crowd of freed prisoners.

"You boys took care of the guards over yonder?" he said.

"No, sir," one said. "They all was already dead."

Jason nodded. He figured as much and turned as one of the men pointed up the street. He saw the warrior standing at the edge of town with a bow in one hand and a rifle in the other.

Cordova sat up and wiped blood from his smashed nose. Jason squatted beside him.

"Mr. Cordova, tell me the name of the man who traded you the Frenchwoman and where I can find him."

Cordova glared at him and shook his head. "You're going to kill me anyway."

"Yes, sir," Jason nodded. "That is a fact."

"Then I have nothing to tell you. I will die with dignity."

"Die, you most certainly will." Jason nodded. "But there will be no dignity for you, Mr. Cordova."

CHAPTER 21

J ASON WIPED THE BLOOD FROM the blade of his buffalo bone knife on Cordova's shirt. He stood and stashed the weapon back into its leg sheath, then backed away from the corpse. After only two minutes of persuasion, Cordova had told him everything he needed to know.

Bret Masters was the man who had raided his home and stolen the woman he loved. He'd find him up on the Arizona-Utah border in a place called Rattler's Bend, not even a hundred miles northwest of Greenville.

Jason learned that Masters regularly raided the four corners area and gathered his human cargo. He usually held them in Rattler's Bend until he had enough prisoners, then he'd make a run down south to the Mexican border to trade them into slavery in exchange for gold or supplies.

Somehow, Jason had thought he'd feel better after killing Cordova. He'd hoped for some feeling of pleasure or relief or some other kind of closure after the dispensation of justice. He looked down at Cordova's dead body, then glanced around. The freed prisoners stared at him, shock and disbelief in their eyes. Maybe they hadn't believed anyone was capable of doing what he'd just done. There was no justice about what he'd done to the man. He started to turn away, but the two axe fighters stepped forward.

"Thank you for helping us, Mr. Peares," the Black man said. "I'm Benjamin Page." He stuck out his hand.

"And I'm Fisher Macmillan," the other said, extending his hand also.

Jason regarded the two men and the elder Indian who stood back from them, but he made no move to return their handshakes. After an uncomfortable few seconds, the men withdrew their hands.

"I didn't come here to make friends with you people," Jason said. He looked at the rest of the freed survivors, maybe two dozen in all. "And I don't care what your names are. I came here for Cordova. Now I'm going after Bret Masters."

"But Masters has my wife," Page said.

"And mine," Macmillan added.

"And my grandson," said the elder Indian.

Jason turned away. "That's your problem. You're free. Do whatever you like. Just don't get in my way."

The woman from the saloon stormed up in front of him, blocking his path. He moved to step around her, his eyes already set on the bleak horizon, his mind calculating a death for Masters that would hopefully be slower and more painful than Cordova's. The woman grabbed his shirtsleeve.

"Masters has my husband too," she said. "If you only wanted to kill Cordova," she said, nodding over her shoulder, "You wouldn't have bothered to help me. You already had what you came for. That man behind the bar would have killed me, and you know it."

Jason said nothing. He just tugged his arm from her, but she yanked back and stared silently at him a moment. Her gaze danced between Jason's eyes, searching for something. Maybe she sought some kind of understanding or sympathy for their situation. He gave her nothing.

"You loved that woman, didn't you?" she said. He said nothing in return, but he couldn't stop his eyes from watering. "Well, I love my man too. I need him back. Please."

"Let him go," Page said. "He don't give a damn about us. He's just like them. Just wants revenge, that's all."

"You can do both," the woman shouted. "You need to kill Masters so bad you can't help us get our families back first?"

Jason ignored her and started to step around her, when suddenly the woman swung at him. She slapped him so hard his teeth banged together. His hat fell from his head, and he stumbled back a step.

He blinked, blinded by a sudden rage. Suddenly, he heard the woman screaming. When the blindness of raw anger passed, Jason realized he held the woman's jaw in his left hand and his gun in his right hand. The weapon was pointed at her face.

Jason composed himself quickly and released her. He took a step backward and started to apologize, but he stopped himself. He wouldn't allow his feelings to interfere with what he had to do. Instead, he simply tucked away his gun and put his hat back on. He walked around her and got his horse from the hitching post by the saloon doorway.

Again the woman placed herself in his path. "Please help us," she said. "Please." She closed her eyes, and her lower lip trembled as she said it one more time. "Please."

The woman's shirt had fallen open, and Jason's gaze trailed along the cuts, scrapes, and bruises that traced from her neck down to her belly and farther, hidden by her skirt.

He stepped around her finally and walked his horse away from the crowd. Then he stopped. He couldn't shake the vision of the woman's tortured body. The physical pain and humiliation she had endured repeatedly at the hands of the bartender and the raiders would pale in comparison to the pain of finding her husband dead or never finding him at all. That kind of pain Jason clearly understood.

For a long time, he said nothing, and his horse waited obediently beside him. He already knew how he would feel when he killed Bret Masters, but still he couldn't let go of the need to see the man die. He knew he'd feel the same emptiness he'd felt watching Cordova die. He'd have no satisfaction, no release of pain or guilt.

Cordova's screams for mercy echoed in his memory. He had

slowly slid the long blade into the man's chest and moved it deliberately side to side while the man gripped his wrist, screaming and grimacing, pleading with him as he tried in vain to stop the cutting. He had imagined the weapon slicing Cordova's evil heart into pieces, and he watched life fade from the man's eyes. When the deed was done, he'd wished he could have made Cordova's pain last far longer than it had.

But what was the point of killing beyond vengeance? He relived Renée's final moments of life for the hundredth time. No amount of killing would bring her back. He suddenly found himself needing a reason to justify killing. There had to be something more than vengeance.

He glanced behind him at the woman pleading for his help. He wanted—no, he needed—to kill Masters and his men for what they'd done, but he also realized their deaths would not ease his own pain. After he killed those men, he'd wander as he did before he'd met Renée, evading the Pinkertons, except now guilt would be his companion.

If he'd gone straight to the cabin after leaving Greenville, Renée would still be alive. If he hadn't wasted three more hours at the cabin napping and feeling sorry for himself, she'd still be alive. If he had read the trail sign closer or picked the right trail. If he had ridden faster. If he hadn't tried to cut that man's throat with a mere belt knife. If he had drawn his gun faster.

Other hostages had died in that canyon with Renée, wives or husbands who couldn't go home to loved ones because of his mistake. If he ignored the cry for help now from these people in his quest for revenge, he'd just be condemning more prisoners to death, or slavery, or both, and he'd carry that guilt with him too. One of the casualties might be the husband of the woman standing behind him.

Jason pushed his hat back on his head and looked around behind him. The small crowd still stared at him. He saw their resolve. They would attempt to find and rescue their kinfolk on their own. They had no choice but to try. He knew they would fail because they could not do what he could. Without his help, these people would never see their loved ones again. They'd die trying, but they'd just be throwing away their lives.

He turned away for a moment and gazed at the warrior who still stood at the edge of the town, waiting for him. Finally, he made his decision. He needed justice, not revenge. Jason had no doubt he would kill Bret Masters and as many of his men as he could find, but only so that other prisoners could live.

He took a deep breath and turned back to the woman.

"What's your name?" he said quietly.

"I'm Samantha Singer," she said. She held her shirt together with her left hand.

He nodded. "We'll try to get your people back, but we have to get organized."

Jason split the gaggle of people into three groups and set them to different tasks. One group collected all the guns and ammunition from Cordova's men in the saloon and the corral. Another group searched all the shacks in town for water jugs and rations. The third group hitched up wagons and saddled up spare mounts.

The teams loaded one wagon with supplies and weapons for the rescue trip up north. Samantha and the elder Indian, who gave his name as Gray Hair Runs No More, rode in the wagon, while Page and Macmillan prepared to ride horseback alongside Jason. The rest of the survivors set out in wagons due southeast, toward their homes.

Gray Hair Runs No More succeeded only partially in translating Arapaho, the warrior's language, for Jason. Still, he couldn't put the warrior's name into a recognizable English translation, though he identified the warrior's mate as Smile of the Little Sunflower.

Two days into the journey, the group crossed a creek, and everyone bathed in the cold water. Several days later, they camped in the rugged foothills three miles west of Rattler's Bend.

After supper, Jason outlined his strategy to everyone so that they'd have hope, so they'd feel like they were part of a rescue plan. They'd hit the outlaw camp hard and furious just before dawn when the guards' attention hit its lowest point.

Jason and the warrior communicated with sign and draw-ings in the dirt, barely visible in moonlight. They decided on a smarter plan, one not involving a suicidal frontal assault. They conferred at length, then slipped into the darkness to reconnoi-ter the outlaw camp.

CHAPTER 22

JASON DIDN'T KNOW IF RATTLER'S Bend got its name because the canyon snaked through the mountain peaks like its namesake or because of the sidewinders who made a mockery of the law and ran home to this natural fortress. He'd heard the town described as an outlaws' paradise, a long, curving canyon sandwiched between nearly vertical, 3,000-foot ridges. It was simply a great hole in the mountains into which only the lawless entered or from which only they emerged.

No sane lawman wanted a criminal bad enough to go into Rattler's Bend. Several had tried and failed. It was said that entire posses had ridden into the great lawless hole in pursuit of criminals, but no one ever saw or heard from them again.

Only the toughest and meanest gunfighters, criminals, and outlaws called the camp home. Equally deadly women lived there also, either outlaws themselves or drawn to the power of the male outlaws. Rattler's Bend had no rules or laws but those a person carried in a holster.

All these thoughts passed through Jason's mind as he and the warrior headed into the darkness toward the enemy camp. He hadn't shared these thoughts with the others. If he did, they would likely lose all hope of ever seeing their loved ones alive again.

Jason followed the warrior in the darkness. They traveled up into the shallow canyon quite a distance from where the rescue team had set up camp. Cresting several rolling foothills, they found a dry creek leading to the wide path that snaked higher into the vertical walled canyon.

They moved slowly and carefully, always watching for look-outs as they neared the outlaw camp. Jason wore the warrior's spare moccasins, soft-soled and uncomfortable for rock climbing but much quieter than boots. He'd left his guns and holsters back at camp and carried only his Winchester, though he prayed he wouldn't have to use it. A gunfight would only invite the same disaster that had cost Renée her life.

The moon sat high in the sky, barely concealed behind the high southern peaks that rimmed the path ahead. The moon edge-lit the clouds high overhead, giving Jason and the warrior just enough light to make their way through the deep shadows of the canyon. A sliver of water trickled through the center of the wide path, winding around brush and small boulders.

Jason began to feel concern. He saw plenty of wagon tracks zigzagging around obstacles on the path and knew they could bring their own wagon up close to the outlaw camp. Even if they managed to free all the prisoners from Rattler's Bend, they'd never be able to make a hasty retreat down the path in the wagon. If they hit one boulder, even a small one, they'd likely lose a wheel.

Jason thought about how to get the prisoners from the canyon over to the rescue camp. Some of the prisoners might be weak or hurt and unable to travel far or fast. They'd never make the treacherous journey up and down the steep paths he and the warrior had followed. Night or day, they'd have to put up a running gunfight, vastly outnumbered by the pursuing outlaws.

They dashed into the brush beside the path when they heard the slow clip-clop of a horse approaching from behind them. Jason aimed his Winchester, then lowered it as the warrior read-ied an arrow in his bow. The rider paused his horse ten paces away and lit up a cigarette. It was a stinky, hand-rolled stogie. *Probably his own personal recipe,* Jason thought as the smoke drifted over to him.

Jason and the Indian froze completely still. Jason knew the

rider might look right at them without seeing them in the darkness. If they made even the tiniest movement, the man's side vision would perceive them as a shadow moving against the background.

The rider sucked deeply, and the embers of his cigarette glowed deep orange for a moment, snapping noisily. He bundled the collar of his coat around his neck, then exhaled the smoke and kicked his horse into a walk again.

The warrior looked at Jason and signed that he would follow the rider. Jason nodded. Whether or not the rider belonged in Rattler's Bend, he would betray the positions of the lookouts since they would either shoot the rider or rise to challenge him.

Jason watched the warrior disappear silently into the darkness. He returned three hours later with bad news. Now Jason understood why entire posses disappeared in Rattler's Bend hunting their criminals.

The rescue group faced no ordinary outlaw camp or hideout. Instead, they had to try to penetrate a mountain fortress—a sizable town in a heavily defended canyon almost a mile long and half a mile wide. The town's forty buildings, mostly log cabins, lay scattered haphazardly across the valley.

The warrior reported seeing 200 horses in four corrals. Huge, sturdy cabins reinforced with extra logs stood at both narrow entrances to the canyon to repel attacks. Extra men stood guard or slept in the fortified cabins. Seven lookouts kept watch at the near entrance, and the same number guarded the far side of the canyon. Dozens of outlaws occupied the town. Rattler's Bend bustled with activity even near midnight. Bret Masters and his outlaws held almost fifty prisoners in four separate shacks located near the center of the canyon. On the far side of Rattler's Bend, the warrior had seen several covered wagons prepared for sunrise departure. Jason knew the prisoners would be moved south for slavery.

At the end of the warrior's silent report etched in the dirt in the dim light, Jason marveled at the completeness of the warrior's picture of what they faced. Then he felt a mild irritation at the man and at the tracking skill he had shown. It was part of the competition they shared. The warrior had sneaked into the mountain fortress unseen and scouted the entire valley, then sneaked out again.

The two men gazed at each other for a moment, and Jason finally gave the man his victory with a simple nod. All of a sudden he was glad the warrior was on his side in whatever situation they would face in the coming day.

It was clear, Jason realized, that an assault on the fortress was impossible. Now he had to lead his rescuers back around the mountains, a trip that would probably take a whole day, maybe more. They had to try to catch the raiders somewhere south, but that would put them down in the flatlands again. An ambush in open land against well-armed outlaws was only slightly less suicidal than assaulting Rattler's Bend.

They made their way back to camp. Jason called everyone together and evaluated the resolve of each person with intense eye contact. No one said anything. They just waited for him to speak.

The wind picked up, and Jason buttoned up his sheepskin coat against the chill. The others also wore coats or heavy wool pullover sweaters or ponchos salvaged from Hell-Town. The warrior and his wife wore heavy buffalo hide wraps.

After a moment, Jason told everyone what they faced. Then he told them of their only option and explained his plan.

CHAPTER 23

THERE'D BE HELL TO PAY when the outlaws discovered the bodies of their lookouts scalped, as if a war party had hit them for trophies. After the warrior had silenced the seven lookouts, Jason helped him with the messy task of removing their hair. He used the buffalo bone knife to follow the warrior's example. They scraped their blades around the men's scalps, then pulled loose the hair with a wet tearing sound. They buried the scalps and left the bodies to be found. Shortly after sunrise, Jason mounted up and simply rode straight into Rattler's Bend.

He wore his double holster as he always did when approaching a town. In addition, he had his two Colts tucked in the front of his belt. He also draped two cartridge belts over his shoulders so they crossed his chest, but with his sheepskin coat unbuttoned and spread open, the cartridge belts were more to increase his sinister appearance than for any practical reason. He looked like any other outlaw gunfighter that might ride into the camp. His reputation was well known throughout the Southwest. It wouldn't take too much of an imagination for anyone to believe he was an outlaw seeking shelter among his own kind.

Jason studied the fortified cabin as he rode past. The warrior's pictorial description hadn't conveyed the invincibility of the structure or the canyon. The walls of the cabin held dozens of sight holes just large enough for a man to aim a rifle through. Such a shooter would be virtually impervious to return fire.

The cabin sat low to the ground, barely six feet high but stretched over thirty feet long. A double thickness of logs comprised the walls and roof of the structure. Even the army would need a lot of dynamite or heavy cannons to break into Rattler's Bend, but the narrow approach would likely prevent that from ever happening.

Jason rode the gauntlet past dozens of rifle barrels. He made it nearly a quarter-mile in before three men walked out of what looked like a saloon to greet him. He did not feel a false sense of security just because he hadn't been shot yet. Catching a glimpse of several sharpshooters on rooftops in his side vision, he knew a dozen rifles tracked his movements.

Jason pulled up beside the men. The eldest stepped forward, pointing his rifle at Jason. The man motioned for him to dismount, so he did. He slid his right boot from the stirrup and stepped down to the left of the horse with a casual tiredness, like he'd been riding all night. He took a deep breath and stretched, then turned to face the man with the rifle.

Without a shred of doubt, Jason knew he faced Bret Masters—the man he had come to kill. With ramrod-straight posture and piercing, sky-blue eyes, the man had a commanding presence. Jason had seen a hundred men like this across the frontier. The man looked fearless, like he was prepared for anything. He had the presence of a man who might have served in the army.

"Give me one reason why I shouldn't kill you right now, mister." He carried the rifle in his right hand and caressed a gun holstered on his left hip.

"Because I didn't come here for trouble. I just need a place to stay for a while."

The man's eyebrows raised in surprise. "Perhaps you haven't heard. This is a closed community." The ridicule was plain in the man's voice.

"I've heard. That's why I'm here. I've got me some disagreeable Pinkerton detectives on my trail a day or two back. I figure they won't come up here after me."

One of the other men spoke. "They won't need to, 'cause you're fixin' to be dead."

The elder nodded at the younger man. "My son, Kyle. I'm Bret Masters. Whom do I have the pleasure of killing today?"

Jason regarded the men for a moment. Masters and his son, both big men, had broad square faces with strong features. Both had short brown hair, neatly shaved mustaches, and both wore clean clothes. Two pairs of deep-set blue eyes studied Jason, though Kyle had a wild youthful look in his eyes. He was about twenty-five or so, Jason guessed. Both men had the same wide-shoulder build, though the elder had lost the tapered look his son possessed. Masters and his son looked like they both held the same low regard for human life.

"If you're asking my name, it's Jason Peares." The corner of the elder Masters's left eye twitched. "Like I said before, I'm not looking for trouble. But if there's to be killing, then we'll all die together."

Jason slowly spread the edges of his coat a bit farther apart so the men facing him would have no misunderstanding about his willingness to grab iron. Several men passed through the entry of the saloon, some wiping their mouths on sleeves. Jason figured the saloon doubled as a place to eat. One of the men moved away from the group and approached.

Masters said, "How'd you get past our lookouts?"

"I saw one man face down in the stream out yonder. He was scalped. I didn't see any others."

Masters glanced to the third man who stood beside Kyle. "Take five men and go find the lookouts. Be careful, there might be a war party out there somewhere."

Bret Masters turned his attention back to Jason. "There's something about you I don't like. All my lookouts are dead just when you happen to ride in here. My gut tells me to kill you, right here and now."

"Yeah," Kyle agreed. "How come you didn't get scalped?"

"I suppose you'll have to ask whoever did the scalping," Jason said. He looked down as if considering all his guns. "But, really, would you try to scalp me?"

He said it nonchalantly, but things weren't developing quite like he'd expected. An outlaw himself, he figured he'd be welcome among a town of outlaws, especially once they knew who he was. He glanced around quickly at bad odds.

Two men faced him and one more approached with four others watching in front of the saloon. Rifles were aimed at him from practically everywhere. Thirty paces separated him from the safety of the saloon cabin, maybe five seconds at a hard run through a hail of hot lead.

He had no doubt he could kill Masters and his son if the discussion deteriorated into gunfire. The warrior, hidden up in the boulders near the canyon entrance, could take out a couple of the men near the saloon, maybe distract the other outlaws long enough so Jason could get to safety. With a lot of luck, Jason might live long enough to grab his last meal before the outlaws stormed the saloon restaurant.

He took a deep breath to steady his nerves and mentally prepared himself for the inevitable gunplay. He glanced from Kyle to Bret Masters. Watched as the elder lowered his rifle, centering it right about where his heart was.

"You're not welcome here, Jason Peares," the man said. "But I ain't gonna kill another outlaw. Our paths might cross again someday, and you can return the favor."

Jason nodded. "Like I said, I'm not here to cause any trouble, but I understand your position. Would it be any problem if I ride out behind those wagons, then?" He nudged his head toward the east end of the canyon where a string of ragged-looking prisoners chained to each other were being loaded into the back of three covered wagons. "The Pinkertons won't be able to pick up my trail if I follow behind them a ways."

Masters nodded, a skeptical look still in his eyes. What Jason really wanted, his only reason to take such a risk and ride into Rattler's Bend, was to find a way to get close to the hostages. Masters had unwittingly given him that opportunity. Killing the man could wait. Sooner or later the man would ride out of Rattler's Bend. When he did, Jason would follow him across the entire Southwest until he found the right opportunity to administer justice.

Jason just turned to mount up when the new man walked up.

"Hold on a minute," the man said.

Jason turned back and froze. He knew the man, and the man knew him. He and Renée had stopped over one night several months before in a cattle camp over in Indian Territory, sometimes called Oklahoma nowadays. The man he now gazed upon had been ramrod on a cattle drive headed north and let them share in a hearty supper as they swapped stories. His name exploded into Jason's memory. Phil Baggerly swaggered forward, smiling devilishly.

"I know exactly why Jason Peares has paid us a visit. I'm just surprised it took so long for him to get here."

CHAPTER 24

"THIS HERE FELLOW SAVED MY hide last year. A couple of US Marshals had the drop on me down at the Freely Ranch in the Texas Panhandle. Jason Peares came along and planted 'em in the ground."

Bewildered by Baggerly's fabrication, Jason kept on his best poker face. Young Kyle Masters gasped.

"You threw down on two US Marshals?"

"As I recall there were four marshals," Jason lied. "Two escaped. Phil never was much good at countin', but he sure is a damn good trail cook."

"Hell, why didn't you say you knew Phil?" Bret Masters said. "Would've saved us all some bad feelings."

Jason quickly fabricated another lie. "What with my reception and all, I didn't want to cause him any difficulties."

"Always the loyal friend," Baggerly said, wrapping an arm around Jason's shoulder. "Bret, this here's a good man to have around in a scrape. How 'bout we fill his belly before we send him on his way."

Bret nodded. "My apologies."

Jason nodded in return. "Can't be too careful who comes around, I suppose."

He stayed in Rattler's Bend only long enough to gulp down a steak with eggs and potatoes on the side, smothered in gravy. He ate alone as the two Masters and Phil Baggerly had other chores to attend to. Afterward, he mounted up and rode slowly up the length of the canyon.

The sheer walls towered overhead. Sunlight already lit the ridgeline of the north face of the canyon. At this time of year, the town might get only four or five hours of direct sunlight.

The stream trickled close to the south wall. All the cabins stood on the relatively flat north half of the canyon floor. On the south half, the ground sloped gently down fifteen feet to the stream. Jason saw indications that the stream could swell over ten times its normal size during rainstorms.

He rode behind the cabins on the high ground, joining up behind the wagon train with Kyle Masters and Phil Baggerly at the east canyon entrance. Two cabin fortresses guarded a much wider space between the sheer cliff walls on that end of the canyon.

Jason pretended not to notice Bret Masters watching him from beside one of the cabins. The man had a gut feeling, and Jason respected that. A leader of men, especially bad men, didn't live to his age without being an accurate judge of character. Perhaps he'd seen some of Jason's seething anger in his eyes. Maybe he was just paranoid because of the line of work he was in. Maybe he just couldn't get past the coincidence of Jason showing up at the outlaw camp just as a load of prisoners was ready to leave. *All good reasons to be paranoid,* Jason thought as he tied a kerchief around his neck and raised it over his nose. He squinted his eyes in the dust kicked up by the wagons and horses in front of him.

Gradually, they wound their way slowly down the canyon stream bed, dodging boulders and scrub brush. The trails they followed later in the day snaked around the low-lying foothills, finally turning to the south where they stopped to rest at the edge of the vast high-desert flatlands. Only a single 300-foot hill lay half a mile off to the west. Kyle Masters kept the caravan moving until late afternoon.

After the break, Jason bade his farewells and headed his horse in a trot for the hill. He rode around the hill out of sight of the caravan, then dismounted. With his Spencer in his right hand and a half-dozen cartridges in his left, he ran toward the peak. When he crawled on his belly to the top and peered into the distance, he found the caravan had begun to move again, now almost half a mile away.

Jason laid his Spencer carefully on the ground. Then he pulled a kerchief from his back pocket and placed the cartridges on the rag. He arranged them neatly, tips even with the edge of the kerchief. He laid himself down on the crest of the hill and got comfortable, then readied the forty-four-inch barrel of the Spencer in front of him. In no big hurry, he removed his coat and made a cushion for his elbows.

Early in the day, Jason had realized Kyle had never let him out of his sight for long. The young man never gave him a chance to talk privately with Phil Baggerly. Bret Masters didn't trust Jason, so he'd tasked his son to keep an eye on him. Yet Baggerly wanted him alive for some reason and had concocted that bizarre story about a shootout with the marshals.

As he peered into the distance through the scope, he saw eight targets to hit—four guards on horseback, three wagon drivers, plus Kyle Masters. The young Masters rode out front, but the guards rode to the left of the caravan. Obviously, there was little need to attend to the chained prisoners, so Jason figured the armed guards rode along for the return trip. They were along to protect the gold they'd get paid in exchange for the prisoners.

He remembered the faces of all of the bad men. Three were Mexican, three were White, and one was Black. Then there was the blue-eyed, square-boned face of Kyle Masters and finally the liar Baggerly who had given Jason credibility and vouched for him in exchange for...what?

Jason prepared himself with practiced patience. His targets couldn't run or hide. At half a mile away, they certainly couldn't shoot back.

He inserted the first cartridge into the chamber and slid the lock closed. The front glass of the scope was calibrated with horizontal marks that Jason knew from practice represented quarter-mile increments that he could use to measure distance.

He placed the lowest horizontal tick mark squarely on Kyle Masters's back, then advanced the vertical line to lead the target. At a muzzle velocity of almost 1,500 feet per second, the bullet would be traveling in the air toward the target for about two seconds. During that time, Masters's horse would move him another eight feet forward. Jason had to account for that movement.

Jason removed his hat and studied the terrain. The grass beside him stood completely still. With no breeze, he didn't have to account for the wind moving his bullet around. Without wind, only gravity affected the heavy ball of metal during its flight.

He took a deep breath and slowly let out half. Completely calm, he squeezed the trigger. The sound exploded in his ear as the stock recoiled hard against his right shoulder. The barrel bounced up slightly, but when it settled back down, he again saw the magnified image of the caravan. Kyle Masters rode casually as before. Unconcerned, Jason turned his attention to the reloading process. The .50-caliber bullet had a long way to travel.

Jason hoped Masters would feel the shock and pain when the bullet slammed into his back and ripped out the front of his chest. He hoped the man would live long enough to scream in agony. Maybe the man would live long enough for Jason to ride back out there and explain to him why he was dying.

Still peering through the scope, he calmly pulled opened the chamber lock lever and ejected the spent shell casing. He inserted a new cartridge and gently slid the lock closed again. The magnified image of Masters's back jerked forward as the bullet slammed him from his saddle.

Quickly, Jason found his next target. The sound of the shot traveled only half as fast as the bullet and the guards would be confused momentarily by Masters's sudden dismount. By the time the sound of the first shot reached them, another man would already be dead by Jason's second shot.

Jason squeezed the trigger a second time, then reloaded and

fired again. He chose his shots carefully. The .50-caliber shell could propel a bullet straight through a man or a horse, and he didn't want to accidentally kill one of the hostages when one of his targets moved in front of their wagon.

Eight targets, eight shots.

One man stopped his wagon and tried to hide behind the wood of the seat. The long-distance bullet splintered through the wood like paper and sent the hiding man tumbling in the dirt. His last target tried to run away by leading his horse beside him as a shield, but Jason simply sighted on the animal's rump and fired. He watched through his sight as his bullet pierced the animal and slammed the last raider to the ground. The dying horse fell across the man's torso.

Jason scanned the area through his rifle scope. None of Kyle Masters's men moved except Baggerly. Jason sighted on the man's back, debating whether or not to let the man live. He watched him throw a ring of keys to a hostage who ventured outside one of the wagons. He decided the man at least earned the right to explain his plans.

After packing away his equipment, Jason rode down to the wagons.

"Mrs. Page?" he asked, scanning the faces. A dark-skinned woman stepped forward.

"You'll be seeing your husband about this time tomorrow." She opened her mouth to speak but made no sound. "Same goes for Mrs. Macmillan and Mr. Singer."

Jason scanned the group. He found a young Indian boy and discovered the young man was the grandson of Gray Hair.

"I'm sure the rest of you also have kinfolk looking for you."

A man moved away from the group and walked toward Jason as he dismounted.

"Is Samantha really alive?" he asked. Jason nodded and Singer fell to his knees. "I thought I had lost her. Only the hope that I might see her again kept me alive."

Jason knelt beside him. "Mr. Singer, you'll see her again real soon, but she's been hurt real bad."

Singer stared at him a moment, then looked at the ground. He closed his eyes and nodded. Jason spoke with some of the freed prisoners, then left the wary group to consider their new and quite unexpected freedom. He walked over to Baggerly, who had wisely moved off a safe distance from the people. About the same age and build as the elder Masters, Baggerly had short gray hair and a weathered look about him.

"So, Mr. Baggerly. You were involved with taking Renée?"

"I was there," Baggerly nodded. "But there was nothing I could do about it. She recognized me. When I approached her at the cabin, she told me she could pretend to be a Frenchwoman. She told me you'd be comin' after her." He added quickly, "It was my word to Bret Masters and Miguel Cordova that kept her...unharmed. A Frenchwoman is worth a lot of money in California."

"So what was the price for a Frenchwoman?"

Baggerly hesitated and looked away. "Three thousand. In gold."

Jason nodded. Absently, he studied the landscape for a moment.

"I have to be honest with you, Mr. Baggerly. I'm looking for a good reason not to kill you."

"I know where she is," he said quickly. "That is to say, I know where they're taking her."

Jason shook his head. "I've already buried her. And I've been to visit Mr. Cordova about the matter. That's how I found you."

Baggerly fidgeted. "I know you've come to kill Bret Masters. I can get you in—"

"I've come to kill all of you." Jason paused and focused his gaze on the man. "And as you've seen, I can get myself in."

"But I can get you out too," Baggerly countered quickly. "Alive."

Jason considered the man's words for a moment, then nodded. "Well, that's a start."

He stared at the man, understanding he'd gotten himself involved in a power struggle between Baggerly and Masters.

"And with Bret Masters dead, you move up in power."

"With him dead, I *am* the power. But if I kill him, it'll just divide the camp and start everyone back-shootin' each other. We both have a lot of loyal followers."

"But if an outsider—an outlaw—kills him, there's no split of loyalty, and everyone follows you."

Baggerly nodded.

"I only see one problem," Jason continued. "Masters is only half the reason I'm here. I also came for the prisoners. These folks tell me there's still a few in Rattler's Bend."

"All right, I'll give you the rest of the prisoners," Baggerly agreed. "Probably four or five of 'em left behind just to work. Too old to fetch a decent price in Mexico."

"And I want an end to your slave trading."

Baggerly shook his head. "I can't promise that. We earn our keep outside the law. It's what we do. Sometimes it's trading, sometimes we hit some banks, maybe cattle and horse ranches, and sometimes it's people. If I don't lead them, someone else will."

Jason nodded. He didn't expect Baggerly to agree on the last account.

"All right, I give you Bret Masters's dead body, you give me the hostages and safe exit." They shook hands.

Constance Morgan jumped into his memory. A month ago, Jason would never have considered hunting a man, even a bad man, to kill as trade for favors. Now Miss Morgan could not only call him a murderer but a bounty hunter as well. That he was doing it to save the lives of prisoners gave him some moral comfort, but not much.

Jason walked off to tend to his horse. Renée had died for $3,000 in gold. Four more hostages had died in his blundered attempt to rescue her. He glanced over at the jubilant survivors. He granted that they were happy to be alive, but for him it was a bitter victory. Had he succeeded in rescuing Renée, though, he would never have gone about rescuing all these people. They'd all be sold into slavery or killed.

No, he thought. *It would have been like Renée to insist we help the others.* Had he been successful in rescuing her, she wouldn't have ridden away without the rest of them.

At sundown, Jason dug a small firepit like he'd seen the Arapaho warrior do. He brewed a pot of strong coffee but didn't eat. The warrior joined him after midnight, bringing with him more bad news.

Riding to check on his mate, the warrior found the Pinkerton detectives had intercepted and interrogated the other freed prisoners who were riding toward tomorrow's rendezvous. The tracks indicated the detectives had spread out around the flatland where the trail came down out of the foothills. They had Jason surrounded and could move in at their convenience, most likely in the morning.

Jason knew he and the Indian could easily escape in the night. Doing so, though, meant he'd have to let Bret Masters live, and he'd have to turn his back on more prisoners who needed saving. Yet the thought of escape merited some consideration.

CHAPTER 25

JASON SIPPED HIS COFFEE AND looked at the warrior. He wondered for a brief moment if the man had ever tried coffee. With the continued expansion of settlers throughout the Southwest, Jason figured in the coming years the native people who survived would be the ones who adapted to a new way of life among the intruders in their lands. Still, there were so many small things that might serve as a constant reminder of the differences between natives and non-natives. It might be the choice of clothing. Maybe methods of worship. Maybe a trivial thing like coffee. Had he ever known an Indian who drank coffee?

None of that mattered in his current situation, though. He thought about his relationship with the warrior. If he gave the word, the man would follow him into the night and help keep him safe from the Pinkertons. He'd make sure the detectives never found their tracks.

The high cost in innocent lives for his own escape was too high.

There was no way Jason would abandon the rest of the prisoners to slavery. If he left the area now, then Renée's kidnappers would go unpunished, and that was completely unacceptable. If he stayed, he'd have to make his stand against the Pinkertons. Either way, more good people would likely die, himself among them.

Jason smiled sadly, then looked at the man and shook his head. He'd seen enough death, and he'd had enough killing and running. The warrior nodded his understanding. Jason dumped his coffee on the tiny fire and lay back, using one of his packs as a pillow. He pulled his hat over his face and slept. What seemed like only a minute later, he heard someone calling his name. It was a woman's voice.

Light peeked around his hat as he opened his eyes. He took a deep breath and sat up. He pushed his hat back up on his head and looked up at Bonnie Drake and another detective. Neither had their guns drawn, probably so they wouldn't upset the nearby prisoners Jason had rescued. It didn't matter much, he reflected. Though he didn't scan the land around the camp, he knew several detectives had him in their rifle sights.

"I honestly didn't expect you'd still be here this morning, Jason," Bonnie said.

"I've been waiting for you," Jason said. "Coffee?"

Bonnie nodded and sat as he set about reviving the fire and brewing a fresh pot. She introduced Jason to Detective Charlie Rodriguez. The men regarded each other without greeting.

The detective was almost as short as Bonnie. He was thick in the chest and hips, with round muscular shoulders and bulging arms that could have belonged to a boxer. Like most Pinkerton detectives Jason had seen, Rodriguez was clean-shaven except for his mustache. They always found time to groom themselves, even out on the frontier. Rodriguez had neat black hair and mustache. The man glanced around uncomfortably.

"Relax, Mr. Rodriguez," Jason chuckled. "If the warrior intended to kill you, he'd have done it already." He indicated the ground opposite the fire. "You're welcome to share my coffee if you like."

Rodriguez nodded and squatted beside Bonnie.

"Besides," Jason continued. "I've always considered sharing coffee as a kind of sacred truce."

Bonnie chuckled. "Never killed anyone over coffee?"

"Coffee is expensive. I'd hate to waste a good cup." They shared a private laugh as if Rodriguez was invisible.

Jason nodded over to the camp where Page, Hamilton, and the others sat reunited with their loved ones.

"You rode in with the wagon?"

Bonnie nodded. "Figured you'd rescue the prisoners, then hit the trail again during the night."

"The thought crossed my mind."

Jason watched the camp prepare a morning meal. Gray Hair sat in quiet conversation with his grandson. The Singers held each other tightly, rocking back and forth. It was as if they'd never let go of one another again. The Pages and Macmillans stood around laughing and hugging each other all over again, as if they awoke to discover the rescue wasn't merely part of some obscene dream. Sunflower sat alone. Bonnie seemed to notice her also.

"So where is the warrior?"

Jason shrugged. The man came and went with the shadows, most times not making a sound unless he wished to be heard. Rodriguez looked around again also.

"He's not a threat, Bonnie." Jason glanced at Rodriguez. "Unless your people start trouble."

Jason fished another cup out of the pack he'd used as a pillow. He poured steaming liquid into the two cups and gave one to Rodriguez and one to Bonnie. She sipped, then handed her cup to Jason to share. Their fingers touched, and they shared a moment of eye contact. He sensed her vulnerability beneath the toughness. He saw the pain of a substantial loss in her eyes.

"I miss her too," he said. Bonnie looked away. "And I know how much it hurts." His eyes watered as did Bonnie's. They were quiet for a long time.

"Why are you still here?" she said finally.

He took a deep breath to compose himself and held it for a moment before exhaling.

"I'm still here because of Miss Constance Morgan, or rather because of what she said to me." He sipped coffee, then handed Bonnie the cup. "There are still four or five prisoners in Rattler's

Bend." Jason paused. "The man who stole Renée from us is there too. He's still alive."

He nodded off to the right where Baggerly had piled the bodies of his brethren together. Neither Baggerly nor any of the freed prisoners bothered to bury the men. Scavenger birds were circling as if waiting for the humans to depart.

He called Phil Baggerly over from his own campfire and shared the plan with Bonnie. When he finished, he noticed the freed captives walking quickly toward him from the wagons, talking excitedly and pointing off into the distance.

Some of the survivors carried weapons taken from their dead captors. They'd just now discovered the Pinkerton sharpshooters. Jason stood quickly, intending to reassure the group he was in no immediate danger, but the crowd of survivors quickly became rowdy. They surrounded him and roughly pushed Bonnie and Rodriguez away.

Tension mounted quickly as Rodriguez went for his gun, but several of the survivors covered the man and Bonnie with their weapons. Jason shoved his way through the crowd, shouting for restraint. He turned his back to Bonnie and Rodriguez, then faced the crowd and told them of his intention to go back to get the other prisoners. Then he'd surrender to Bonnie Drake.

Page pulled a spyglass from his back pocket and extended its length.

"I got this from one of the outlaws' horses." He scanned all the mounted detectives, then whistled. "Looking at how they're armed, I'd say they have little intention of accepting your surrender. I count ten of 'em. All armed to the teeth."

Bonnie tried to step forward, but someone pushed her back. "It's just a precaution, Jason."

"Understandable," Jason said. "But let's keep this under control. I don't want anybody getting killed on account of a little misunderstanding."

"Mr. Peares," Rodriguez said. "We're taking you in dead or alive. There's no need for anyone here to get hurt." He raised his voice. "And I suggest you folks don't interfere with the law."

A tall, wiry man detached himself from the crowd around Jason and approached Rodriguez. His suit was tattered and filthy, and his long brown hair was frazzled, his mustache and beard equally unruly.

"May I see your papers, sir?"

"Papers?" Rodriguez regarded the man. "And who might you be?"

"Thadius P. Hornton, sir. I'm an attorney in Santa Fe, New Mexico."

Rodriguez eased his hand away from his gun and reached into his open coat. He retrieved a folded piece of paper, which he handed to Hornton. The attorney read for a while, nodding to himself. Finally, he looked up at the detective. Hornton smiled and glanced at the people around him, then at Jason.

"Sir, you are not the law," Hornton said, handed the paper back to Rodriguez. "And our interfering with the activities of an employee of a private company is not illegal. We are well within the bounds of our civil rights by preventing you from taking this man into custody."

Rodriguez hesitated, thinking. "We're taking this criminal in, mister."

"Alleged criminal, sir," Hornton said. "He has not had a trial yet."

Rodriguez hesitated and Jason said, "Mr. Hornton, I'd say you've got 'em outmaneuvered. If anyone ever says anything bad about attorneys, I'll have words with them." He took a deep breath and looked at Bonnie. "It doesn't matter, though. I made my decision last night. I'm going back to Rattler's Bend to get those prisoners. And I'm going to kill Bret Masters. When I'm done, you can have me."

Bonnie stepped forward. "Have you?" she repeated skeptically.

He nodded. "I'm tired of running. Everywhere I go people die." Rodriguez started to protest, but Jason waved him quiet. "There's only two ways in or out of Rattler's Bend. This trail is one way, the other is a day's ride that way." He nodded to the west. "I'm going back to get those people. You're welcome to ride along. Either accept it or pull that gun."

Rodriguez looked like he wanted to settle the issue, but Bonnie Drake defused the tension. She accepted Jason's terms.

"I'll ride with you," she said. "Two of my men will escort the prisoners over New Mexico way and see that they get home safe."

Bonnie sent Rodriguez out to inform the other detectives. Jason wasted no time packing to leave. He gave no farewells to the people he'd rescued. He simply mounted up and started back to the north.

After a time, Baggerly took over leading the small caravan, followed closely by Jason and Bonnie Drake. Sunflower rode at the rear, leading the warrior's pony and their pack mules. An hour after they departed, Jason saw Bonnie staring behind him. He looked back and saw the warrior riding alongside his woman.

Jason caught her eye when she turned back forward.

"He was hiding behind that little puff of grass right next to where you sat drinking coffee." They laughed.

The trip back up into the mountains took the better part of a day. Jason called a halt when they joined the wide stream bed leading into Rattler's Bend. Darkness would arrive quickly, so he decided to ride in just after sunrise the next morning.

Jason looked back along the trail and saw the Pinkertons following a mile back. He set up camp and told Bonnie where to have her men wait.

"If anybody but me comes down that trail, don't ask any questions. Just start shooting. And for heaven's sake, don't try to come in there after me." He explained the fortifications at the canyon entrance. "If I don't come out of there, you can be sure I'm dead."

She started to mount up to leave but hesitated with her foot in the stirrup.

"Jason," she said. "There's something I have to tell you."

He held up his hand. She looked like she was fixin' to get all emotional on him.

"Save it for later," he said. "I don't need any distractions right now."

"I won't be around later," she said.

Bonnie reached into her coat pocket and pulled out a crumpled piece of folded paper. She held out the note to him, but for some reason he couldn't make his arm move. His gaze flicked from the note to Bonnie, but she wouldn't meet his eye.

"What's this?" Finally, he took the paper.

"This is all my fault." She paused. "I'm resigning. I just had to see you again before I left for home."

Without any further explanation or even a farewell, Bonnie mounted her horse and raced off down the trail. Jason watched her awhile, then he unfolded the paper. As he read the letter he gasped, unable to breathe. His legs wobbled and crumbled beneath him. He fell to his knees. He read the letter a second time, then a third. He tried so hard to hold back the tears that his whole body began to tremble. He dropped the note and covered his face with his hands. He leaned over until his head rested against the ground, his hat flattened under his forehead.

"Dear God in heaven. What have I done?"

CHAPTER 26

J ASON, PHIL BAGGERLY, AND THE warrior and his wife set up camp to the side of the wide stream bed. Unlike the other trail he'd used to enter Rattler's Bend, no water trickled down this trail. Jason started their campfire within clear sight of the Pinkertons. Mostly, he didn't want them wondering where he was, nor did he want them trying to sneak up to find him. Besides, there was nowhere for him to go except into Rattler's Bend since the detectives' camp protected the downhill approach to the trail.

Jason removed his gun belt and spent the evening hours meticulously cleaning his pistols and Winchester rifle. He tended to his Spencer long rifle also but knew he wouldn't need it in Rattler's Bend. He loaded his weapons and stuffed extra cartridges in his gun belt, then watched curiously as the warrior performed his own preparations.

He knew little of Indian ways of war. He never even considered that a warrior had to do more than just stick his arrows in a pouch to be ready for battle. He'd heard war stories from other frontier people, though he'd never really encountered the true natives of the land during anything more than infrequent trading, certainly never in battle.

Mostly, he figured Indians had peaceful traditions. Most tribes were friendly and unpretentious, until the unending westward tide of settlers began to displace them from their land and the army declared war on them.

When riled up for war, the native people were deadly opponents. Jason had heard many stories of how warriors could slither unseen through prairie grass and right into the encampments of their enemies. In broad daylight, they could kill a guard or sentry with an arrow so quietly that no one ever knew where the hidden attacker lay.

Now, Jason felt a shiver embrace his spine as he watched the warrior check and adjust the tension on his bow. The man sorted his arrows into two different stacks in front of him. Jason understood his new friend a little better. Just as he used different guns or rifles for specific situations, the warrior also used a variety of weapons to do his work.

One of the arrows, simply a long, thin reed-like shaft, was tapered to a sharp point on one end with no arrowhead. A five-inch black feather was tied to the tail end. Jason guessed the feather kept the lightweight arrow stable as it traveled through the air toward its target. Jason had been shot and stabbed a time or two over the years. Yet he still had trouble imagining the terrible pain a man might feel as a thin arrow, such as the one he now looked upon, pierced his chest or back.

Phil Baggerly concentrated on the weapons also, and Jason saw understanding in his eyes. He obviously had specific knowledge of the ways and weapons of the warrior.

"The thin one you're looking at there," Baggerly said with a nod at the stack of pointed arrow shafts. "It's a lightweight, short-range weapon. That one can pierce straight through a man and come out the other side if shot with enough force."

Jason caught the warrior's eye and gestured toward the second type of arrow. The man nodded and handed one to Jason. Its shaft was longer and thicker than the lightweight weapon. Baggerly continued his discourse.

"Now that one's much heavier, made for silent, long-distance kills. It's the equivalent of a sharpshooter's weapon, and he can kill a man from a few hundred paces, maybe more."

Jason studied the two-inch, triangular arrowhead tied to the tip of the shaft. It was paper-thin, narrowed to a point at the tip, and wide at the base. The arrowhead shone in the firelight.

"That's obsidian," Baggerly continued. "It's a black volcanic rock. Razor-sharp, too, more like glass than rock. I've seen some pieces worked sharper than any steel knife blade. He's carved some other arrowheads from thin pieces of fire-hardened wood. It looks like he's whittled those with super-sharp edges too."

Jason realized the thin obsidian arrowhead would slice through internal organs and cut through hard bones until finally slamming to a stop somewhere inside the target's body. Even if the victim survived the initial penetration, he would be immobilized by the shock of indescribable pain.

Then he examined one of the arrows with a thicker arrowhead carved from the fire-hardened wood. It was a particularly nasty-looking weapon. Because of its thickness, the arrow wouldn't penetrate very far into its target, probably only far enough to puncture a man's lungs or lodge into his heart. The razor-sharp arrowhead would remain imbedded in its victim if the shaft was pulled out. Because of the shape of the arrowhead and its thick base, it would be impossible to remove without having a doctor to cut it out.

Jason felt a shiver up his spine as he examined the deadly weapon in the firelight. Phil Baggerly stared at it also. Jason looked at the Indian and smiled as he put the arrow back in its place. The barest hint of a smile cracked the warrior's countenance, and he nodded toward Baggerly.

"Mr. Baggerly," Jason said. "I dare say he plans to serve you one of these little monsters if you don't hold up your end of the bargain."

The warrior placed each type of arrow in its separate pouch in his quiver. Then he laid the quiver neatly next to his bow. On top of the quiver, he carefully arranged six small throwing knives and two larger knives for close combat. The warrior had a wider variety of weapons than Jason had.

The three men sat in silence for some time. Baggerly prepared for sleep first. The warrior put out the fire, then carried his weapons into the darkness to join Sunflower in their bedroll. Jason wrapped himself in his heavy blanket. As always, he slept with a gun on the ground near his head. He listened to the night sounds for a long time and thought about the letter that had shattered his reality and exposed the truth about the lie that was Renée-Simone. Or Renée Shelley. Or Shelley Drake.

Jason had told Bonnie Drake he didn't want any distractions, but she'd handed him Renée's letter anyway. Now he tried to push the letter from his mind and find sleep. He thought about the Arapaho warrior. Ironically, Jason had only one friend in the whole world but couldn't even pronounce or translate the man's name.

Jason awoke long before the sky lightened but lay still until he heard the warrior stir. They got up together. Each moved away into the rocks to do their private business. Afterward, Jason prepared a pot of coffee and nudged Baggerly awake with his boot. Then he rechecked his weapons and strapped on his gun belt. When he turned around, he saw the warrior also ready for battle.

When Baggerly had finally collected himself, he helped himself to some coffee.

"Where's your Indian friend?"

Jason looked around and shrugged. He had turned his back for a moment, and the warrior had disappeared.

They broke camp and left Sunflower to ride south alone. Jason rode slowly along the stream bed trail toward Rattler's Bend, leading the warrior's pony behind him. He followed Baggerly higher into the mountains. They passed ten lookouts along the last mile before the canyon entrance. Then they rode by the twin fortified cabins. Baggerly led him along the creek, by the south cliff, and up the bank onto the flatland of the canyon floor. They headed over to the saloon restaurant where Bret Masters waited in front, rifle in hand.

Phil Baggerly rode away to the right, signaling to approaching outlaws as he passed them. He shouted some commands, and Jason was pleased to see that the men and women gathering around lowered their weapons. He'd still had a lingering doubt about Baggerly's trustworthiness, but the man apparently had control over the outlaws. They just watched as Jason rode by. It was one less thing for him to worry about.

Jason paused about twenty paces from the saloon and dismounted. The canyon was still in shadow, though the sky was lighting up fast. Despite the morning chill, he kept his coat open so he could make a fast draw for his guns. He knew he would need to very soon.

He looked around at the dozens of outlaws gathering to watch the spectacle. He had walked right into the nest of snakes. Only Baggerly's control over the outlaws would keep him alive. Only Jason's own actions in the next few seconds would keep Baggerly in control.

Baggerly had warned him that Masters could quickly gather a handful of loyal gunmen when he discovered Jason had returned. As Jason walked closer to Masters, he saw five of his men. The tip of a rifle poked over the edge of the saloon roof. Jason saw a man's hat behind the barrel. Two men stepped into view from the far side of the cabin wall, and a shadow moved in the doorway of the saloon restaurant.

Jason stopped several paces short of Masters and flexed his right gun hand. He briefly considered how he would draw, but the most effective way seemed also the most reasonable. He could outdraw most men with his left-hand draw, but his right-hand draw was a shade faster than his left.

Brett Masters stepped sideways from the saloon doorway to face him. He worked the lever on his rifle to chamber a round.

"Where's my son?"

"Gettin' his bones picked clean right about now, I reckon." Jason paused for effect. "You remember the Frenchwoman?"

Masters nodded. "I shoulda killed you when I had the chance."

"True. But you have another chance now."

Jason saw no fear in Masters's eyes. Instead, he recognized the confident look he often encountered with renegade military men when they knew they'd scored a strategic victory over their enemy. He had Jason outgunned, and they both knew it.

Bret Masters raised the rifle in his right grip. At the same time, he grabbed the gun holstered on his left hip.

CHAPTER 27

ASON AND THE WARRIOR HADN'T wasted time discussing possible strategies. Instinct told Jason the man would select a high vantage point where he could cover the entire kill zone. He'd be on one of the cabin roofs near the saloon restaurant or up in the boulders on the north side of the valley.

When Masters moved for his pistol, Jason drew both his guns and crouched to throw off Masters's aim. The other gunmen reacted when their leader drew.

The shooter on the roof leaned up to get a shot. He took aim and showed his head—a small target for Jason to hit at twenty paces, even under the best of circumstances. Jason ignored him. He knew the Indian would take out the roof shooter first since he was Jason's hardest target.

The warrior attacked from the pine trees by the stream to Jason's left. He made the perfect kill shot from over two hundred yards away. The arrow pierced the rooftop shooter high in his back between the shoulders as he lay prone, cutting deep down into his chest. When the shooter on the roof screamed in agony, the two gunmen hiding behind the saloon wall hesitated for a moment. One looked up briefly to see what had happened.

Jason fired his first shot at Bret Masters, aiming for his gun hand. He wanted the outlaw leader alive, at least for a while. In the same motion, he fired his second shot at the man aiming from the saloon doorway. Both his shots missed, but the door jamb exploded in splinters. The man ducked instinctively, and Jason's third shot plugged him squarely in the face.

Jason's fourth shot shattered Masters's left arm just above the elbow and turned him sideways a bit so he couldn't bring his rifle to bear immediately. Another arrow slammed into one of the two remaining gunmen, knocking him into the other. Jason took careful aim and shot twice at the last gunman.

Masters finally spun back around to bring his rifle to bear just as an arrow slammed into him. The man's eyes widened in surprise, and his mouth opened as if to scream, but he made no sound.

In the space of five seconds, Jason had fired six quick shots. The brief gunfight began and ended without Masters or any of his men getting off a single shot. Jason had expected more of a challenge, but he always took his victories any way he could. Fact was, he had help this time. Otherwise, the outcome might have been quite a bit different.

Glancing around, Jason stood and holstered his guns, mentally counting how many shots he had left in each gun—two in the right gun, four in the left, and five each in his two belt guns. He walked over to Masters, heard the shooter on the roof still squirming around up there, howling in pain. The man finally tumbled over the edge and fell to the ground, an arrow shaft angled high in his upper back. He landed awkwardly on his head. Jason heard a crack, but he wasn't sure if it was the arrow shaft breaking or the man's neck.

Bret Masters struggled to remain standing, and he wavered on unsteady legs as Jason stopped in front of him. The warrior's final arrow had ripped through Masters's right arm as he brought his rifle up. The arrow had pinned the man's arm against his side. The outlaw still held the rifle in his grip. He groaned and distorted his face with the painful effort to point the weapon. He fumbled the rifle, finally dropping it to the ground.

Jason could only see about six inches of the arrow shaft protruding from the man's arm. The rest of the thirty-inch shaft was buried deep inside his chest. Jason examined the tail end of the thick shaft. One of the nasty ones, he observed with satisfaction. The fire-hardened arrowhead had probably punched clean through Masters's heart and both lungs.

Masters stumbled toward Jason as if to attack, his right arm pinned and his left arm dangling helplessly. Jason simply grabbed him under the chin and looked at him a moment. He pushed Masters back and kicked at his legs. The man stumbled and fell onto his back. The man squirmed and trembled in pain, coughing up blood and gasping for breath. Then he wet his pants and lost his bowels. As with Cordova, there was no dignity in death.

Jason knelt beside Masters and grabbed him by the chin again. He forced the man to look at him.

"I'd wager you're in a fair amount of pain," Jason said. "Like her last few moments of life."

The outlaw leader opened his mouth to say something but only made pathetic croaking sounds. Every attempt to breathe, to suck air into his ripped-apart lungs, made him gasp louder.

Jason watched Bret Masters die slowly. He saw the terrible pain etched across the man's face, saw the distorted grimace wrinkle his features, and watched his eyes roll up until only the whites were visible. Bret Masters died with his eyes wide open, his face frozen in pain. Jason let go of his chin and stood. Then he turned to find Phil Baggerly standing a short distance behind him. The new outlaw leader stepped forward and glanced around at the dead outlaws.

"Very nicely done," he said quietly so only Jason could hear.

In the distance behind Baggerly, Jason saw three elder people.

"I thought there were four or five prisoners."

Baggerly nodded. "I was told there were four. One died two nights ago." In a loud voice for all to hear, he added. "You got what you came for, and he got what he deserved. Now it's time for you to leave. You ain't welcome here."

Jason didn't argue. He knew Phil Baggerly had to establish control and leadership quickly in front of his outlaws. Jason obeyed and walked over to his horse. He grabbed the reins and led his animal and the Indian's pony over to the prisoners. Baggerly called out to him.

"Jason Peares," he said. Jason stopped and turned. "Don't go thinkin' we're friends or associates or anything like that. I see you around here again, you're a dead man."

Jason nodded and continued over to the three prisoners. Two of the elder prisoners showed the body language of a married couple. Jason helped them onto his horse and told the elder Black man to get on the pony. They looked confused, but he told them they had their freedom if they kept quiet and did what he said. He led them to the east end of the canyon. Again he passed the fortified cabins and the lookouts, then made his way slowly out of Rattler's Bend forever.

Three hours later, Jason approached the bend in the trail where he'd made camp the night before. This time he passed the campsite and led the prisoners down the trail a ways toward the Pinkerton camp. Rodriguez and three other detectives stood waiting, rifles aimed at him. Jason knew the other detectives would be hidden in the rocks on both sides of the trail.

Rodriguez stepped forward.

"Jason Peares. I'm taking you into custody. You can come peaceable or not."

CHAPTER 28

J ASON LAY ON THE FLOOR of his empty jail cell, stretched out on the thin rag blanket that served as his bedroll. He could feel the ground's coolness through the material, comforting during the day, too cold at night. He'd measured the tiny cell with his boots and found it to be four feet by five. There was just enough room for him to lay stretched out diagonally corner to corner.

Four adobe brick walls without windows enclosed him. Only a twelve-inch square hole in the thick hardwood door gave him light or sound from the world outside his cell.

By some odd turn of events that he didn't quite understand, Jason found himself hauled all the way to Santa Fe, New Mexico. It had been a hot and torturous ride in a poorly ventilated, steel-reinforced stagecoach that rode on bad springs. Rodriguez apparently hadn't appreciated his previous dispatch of the half-dozen Pinkerton detectives who had tried to kill him, so he had Jason hog-tied. His hands were shackled behind his back and were chained to his feet and to the floor of the coach with huge padlocks. His body was bruised from head to toe from enduring the entire three-day trip lying on one side or the other on the coach floor.

Rodriguez seemed to think his case was too important for any of the county precinct courts. The man said his trial belonged in the First District Court in New Mexico.

One of the other detectives said he wished Jason would've

put up a fight. Had he done so, he would've made it easy on the Pinkertons so they could just dump his body with the nearest deputy or sheriff. They could've just signed witness papers and got back home to their families. If Jason had known the law would take six weeks to get his trial done with, he never would have surrendered.

Strangely, he missed Bonnie Drake. She'd left the other detectives before Jason returned from Rattler's Bend. He didn't see her at the trial, nor did she visit him in jail. She was his last connection with Renée, and he had wanted to see her one last time. After reading the letter she'd given him, he understood why she'd quit the Pinkerton Agency and why she couldn't see him.

Renée flashed through his memory often. When he closed his eyes, he could see her long, silky-brown hair, cream-colored skin, and gentle smile with full lips. Those pretty light-brown eyes still stared at him, even from the grave. In a perfect world he would have married her. They would have had children together. Instead, he'd ended up tracking down the men who had killed her. He'd murdered them like they murdered her.

Jason sighed out loud to his empty jail cell. He thought about Miss Constance Morgan and finally admitted to himself what he'd really done. He'd murdered men in cold blood. There was no doubt about it. Whether he was getting his own revenge or saving prisoners wasn't really the point. He'd have gone back for Bret Masters even if no prisoners had remained in Rattler's Bend. He'd taken the law into his own hands the same way Sanderville's Pinkertons tried to in Franklin Town.

He could have escaped after leaving Rattler's Bend. He could have abandoned his mount after pointing the way for the three elderly survivors and then fled afoot into the mountains with his warrior friend. With that man's help, Jason knew he could learn to live off the land indefinitely.

Rodriguez and his detectives would have continued to hunt him, though. Eventually, he and the warrior would've had to kill those frontier detectives too. He figured most of those men had wives and children. If he killed those men, he'd be wrecking more families.

So instead he'd surrendered. He'd been on the run from the law for over seven years. Now he wanted nothing more to do with that outlaw life. Nor could he envision a life without Renée. At least now there would be no more killing.

Almost fifty prisoners were free and had returned to their families because of Jason. He took a measure of comfort in that knowledge. He remembered the looks of sadness on the faces of the first group of prisoners he'd rescued when he said he was going to surrender to the Pinkertons. He recalled the looks of gratitude on the faces of the last three elderly prisoners. The memory reassured him that he'd done the right thing.

Rodriguez had stepped toward Jason on the trail and stuck the business end of his Winchester Yellowboy against Jason's chest. The man looked like he was silently begging Jason to make a move for his guns. Jason had turned his back on the detective and helped the old couple down from his horse instead. The woman hugged him wordlessly for a long time before walking over to the other detectives with her husband. The old Black man slid down from the pony, placed an understanding hand on Jason's shoulder, and thanked him. Jason gazed into the man's green eyes a while and found solace there.

Still facing away from Rodriguez, he pulled his two Colts from his belt and stuck them into a pocket in his saddlebag. He did the same with his holster guns, then packed away his gun belt. Jason ground-tied the warrior's pony to a large stone, then he untied the buffalo bone knife from his leg and placed it carefully atop the same stone, a clear message for the warrior not to interfere. After that, he simply mounted up and waited for Rodriguez to produce a rope to tie his hands.

News about Jason's capture had spread quickly, the Santa Fe sheriff told him. The town's population swelled by several hundred as people flocked to see the notorious gunfighter hang. Most left disappointed, he said, because the historic trial was delayed several weeks until Sheriff Townsend could arrive from Malden, Missouri, to present his personal evidence.

People came from all over the region. Politicians and newspaper reporters came from major cities. Spectators and lawmen came from all over the Southwest. Even a few people who had a personal interest in seeing Jason's demise journeyed all the way from back East. Others just wanted to get a glimpse of the infamous outlaw Jason Peares.

By the end of the fourth week, the whole event had lost its excitement. Most of the folk who expected to see a quick hanging just packed up and went home. Still, the sheriff relayed daily requests from people who wanted to visit Jason—folks who claimed to know him personally or who had ridden with him on a trail or cattle drive. Reporters tried to visit too, but Jason knew they just wanted to chronicle his outlaw deeds in a book for which they would undoubtedly make a handsome income.

Jason refused them all. He took no visitors except for his attorney. Thadius P. Hornton offered to represent him at his trial, but he politely told the man to go back home. There was no way they'd win the case, he told the attorney. It was impossible for a gunfighter with his reputation to get a fair trial. It would be nothing more than a formality, a waste of a day in court plus a waste of Hornton's money for travel expenses. The attorney took the case anyway and the trial lasted six whole days.

To Jason's surprise, Hornton brought dozens of people to the witness stand to testify to Jason's good deeds. Nearly half of the hostages he had freed journeyed to Santa Fe to speak on his behalf. The Pages, the Singers, and the Macmillans all testified how he'd saved them from slavery or certain death. The attorney produced favorable evidence, factual and circumstantial, relating to virtually every gunfight Jason had over the years. Hornton expertly portrayed Jason Peares as a victim of his own skill with the gun, not the vicious killer people believed him to be.

Hornton painted the picture that Jason drifted continuously, never stopping long enough to enjoy a homestead and family like most other people. He portrayed him always running from those who hunted him. He killed only when couldn't avoid a fight. His reputation as a gunfighter attracted hunters who intended to kill him, and he relied on his gun skills to survive.

Hornton stated that Jason Peares reacted the way any normal man would react given the same life-threatening situations. "In the circumstances of most of his gun battles," Hornton said, "self-defense could be reasonably applied as a legal defense. In other gunfights, Jason merely defended people unable to defend themselves. He was a hero of the defenseless."

Hornton even found witnesses to some of his gunfights with lawmen or bounty hunters. People described him as a reluctant participant, forced to use his deadly skills in a fight his opponents would not allow him to turn away from.

At the end of the sixth day of final arguments and presentations by the defense and prosecution, Hornton confided to Jason that he believed he'd successfully planted a reasonable doubt in the judge's mind. A tiny part of Jason's mind held onto the hope that he would not be hanged.

In chains that bound his hands behind his back and to his ankles, Jason waited in a side room for two hours with only Hornton and his ever-present armed guard for company. Finally, the sheriff called them back into the courtroom.

As he dragged his chains into the silent room, Jason regarded the silent audience. They all stared at him. About a hundred people crowded into a space normally reserved for less than half that many. Though separated from Jason by a waist-high wood railing, the people in the front row could have reached out and touched his back when he sat in front of them.

Jason faced the judge's raised podium from half a dozen paces. He sat squished between the burly armed guard and Thadius P. Hornton at a rickety, desk-like table built for two. He glanced over to the single tiny window in the left wall. The glass pane was blurred with too much dirt for him to see anything outside.

When the elderly judge hobbled into the courtroom from a side door, everyone stood in respect. He slowly climbed the two steps and sat behind the podium. Then he motioned for every-one to sit. He contemplated Jason awhile, then the audience, searching for words to express his thoughts. Behind him, Jason could feel the tension building in the courtroom, as if everyone held their breath.

The old man looked wise. Thin wisps of white hair stretched sparsely across the top of his head. Brown age marks speckled his face and showed through the hairs on the nearly bald dome of his head. His steady hands were bony and his skin mottled, but his face was hard and lean, blue eyes clear and intelligent.

Jason felt comfortable with the man's thoughtful approach to the trial. Though the man—Hubert Tomlinson was his name—rarely spoke throughout the trial, he always asked appropriate and intelligent questions.

Hornton said Tomlinson had deliberated many legal argu-ments and had made important case law over the years. He held an esteemed reputation as a fair and honest man who lifted himself above popular opinion or influence. Jason believed he would actually receive a fair decision from the judge. Even more, he clung to the very slim possibility that he would be acquitted and set free.

CHAPTER 29

"**J**ASON PEARES," THE JUDGE BEGAN. Jason returned the man's gaze and stared directly into his blue eyes.

"You stand accused of twenty-six counts of murder. You have killed law officers, duly registered bounty hunters, and detectives of the Pinkerton National Detective Agency, all of whom sought to uphold the law and bring you to justice."

Judge Tomlinson paused and looked around the room. His posture changed slightly, suggesting to Jason the judge was done talking directly to him.

"However," he said to the audience. "I must confess to being deeply concerned by the degree of bias in the general population regarding this case. I admit that I too was convinced this trial would be merely a formality in a simple case that would result in a quick conviction and hanging.

"But the defense counsel has presented evidence which depicts a rather different description of the circumstances and the charges against the accused. On one hand, the activities of the accused resulted in the death of twenty-six citizens over the past seven years—citizens supposedly engaged in the pursuit of justice. I won't even begin to speculate how many lawless citizens have died by Jason Peares's guns.

"Recently, however, his deadly deeds resulted in the salvation of a great many civilians imprisoned by heartless outlaws, and he also brought frontier justice to those murderous men."

The judge paused and took a sip of water from the glass near his left hand. "In general, one might think killing in self-defense is a simple issue. Certainly, if the assailant is a thief or other lawless person intent on doing harm, then one might justify or even sympathize with the killing of that person.

"But what if the assailant is an officer of the law or wears a badge that represents the interests of the law, as in the case of the Pinkerton detectives? And what if the alleged criminal is hunted by these citizens, like game, simply because he has a price on his head?

"How can one argue murder rather than self-defense, especially when witnesses indicate that all the hunters clearly stated they had no intention of taking him alive for a trial?"

Jason nodded in response to the judge's reasoning. He liked the direction the man was taking with his explanation.

"These are the complicated questions that must be considered to arrive at a fair decision as to the disposition of the accused. I must also consider the far-reaching implications that today's decision may have on future cases. I would hope that everyone present can appreciate the difficulty of my task.

"Jason Peares, are you a killer?" Judge Tomlinson asked rhetorically. He made direct eye contact again.

"There is no doubt in my mind that you are indeed." He waved his hand lightly through the air as if dismissing the point.

"Of course, the very same can be said of many bounty hunters, Pinkerton detectives, or even lawmen. In fact, the weapon skills you possess and the courage you recently displayed against overwhelming odds are the very skills we require and respect among our honorable lawmen and soldiers in uniform."

He paused and sipped more water, then he spoke again to the audience. "With great emotion, I have gazed into the eyes of people who would have perished but for this man's deadly skills." The judge pointed a gnarled finger at Jason.

"So, you can see my dilemma. If a US Marshal did what the accused has done for the victims here in this room, he would be hailed as a hero. From what I've learned from these victims, though, I doubt even a dozen lawmen could have saved these people. How then do we hail the accused? Is he a hero or a murderer?"

Judge Tomlinson looked at Jason. "Are you an outlaw?" he asked. "Undeniably. I won't pretend to understand the lifestyle of the outlaw, though I suspect it isn't pleasant. But I must consider the broader question."

Tomlinson addressed the audience again. "Did the accused choose to live outside the law or did the letter of the law unjustly compound his situation by removing his choice? If he freely chose life outside the law, then he most certainly must accept the consequences and the responsibility for his actions, whether or not he saved lives during his journeys.

"Society turns a blind eye and a deaf ear when a citizen rids the land of a lawless or predacious criminal, whether by lawful means or otherwise. But society understandably demands retribution if a citizen kills an officer of the law under virtually any circumstance."

Jason stifled a yawn, gritting his teeth together with the effort to keep his mouth closed. Out of the corner of his eye, he saw a movement. He looked up and saw a wasp-like insect slowly fly across the ceiling near the wall behind the judge. It bumped into the wall frequently, as if feeling blindly as it flew along. It finally reached the far right corner of the room and stuck itself to the ceiling.

Jason tried to focus on what the judge said, but his attention drifted. Though he'd never had occasion to witness any lawmaking, he'd heard many stories over the years from people who'd sat through trials.

Judges, especially the old and learned ones, seemed to feel that educating the audience was part of their job. Sometimes they tended to ramble, as this judge seemed destined to do. Jason shook his head and forced himself to pay attention.

The judge commented on the doubt the defense had planted in his mind. He seemed particularly sensitive to Jason's lack of choice in accepting outlaw life and especially knowing he wouldn't get a fair trial in Malden. The prosecution had not proved Jason did anything more than kill in self-defense the men, lawmen or otherwise, who sought to kill him merely to collect a handful of gold.

Sheriff Townsend proved that Jason had killed four of the men who murdered his family. Hornton didn't argue the fact. The men had picked a fight, and Jason sure enough had shot them dead.

Townsend also presented proof that Jason had killed a fifth man, an unarmed deputy, in the same shootout that night, which surprised Hornton. Jason had forgotten to mention the information that Renée had told him. The sheriff produced signed testimony from witnesses who said he turned and shot an unarmed deputy when they came to arrest him.

Jason looked across the room at Sheriff Townsend. The man sat under the dirty window in the gated area reserved for witnesses. He hadn't changed much in seven years. Tall and stocky, about fifty now, he still looked about 250 pounds. He was mostly muscle, except for a gut that had filled out considerably over the years. Short gray hair framed his square face. A neatly trimmed mustache accentuated the sneer that still puckered his lips. Squinty, mischievous eyes framed by prominent crow's-feet still taunted Jason. Townsend worked his mouth like he had seven years ago, as if chewing on an invisible piece of straw. His massive square jaw jutted forward. His attitude made him look snobby, superior.

Jason looked back to the judge, knowing somehow the man would separate fact from fiction, see through all the lies and set him free. The judge continued his legal discourse.

"I cannot in good conscience convict the accused of murdering the men who killed his family any more than I can convict him of killing hunters who intended to kill him and who intended to deny him an appropriate surrender or a fair trial. But I'm troubled by the revelation that the accused allegedly shot the deputy without provocation. Everything I've heard about this young man has convinced me he would not kill an innocent or unarmed man in cold blood, not today nor seven years ago."

Jason glanced over at Townsend. The sheriff's sneer disappeared, replaced by a look of concern. Hornton had questioned why the sheriff didn't respond with deadly force if Jason really shot an unarmed deputy. Why would a deputy respond to a shooting without arming himself? In fact, why didn't Jason just continue his shooting spree and kill the sheriff as well? The prosecution's answer to the challenge was that Jason had simply run out of bullets in his gun.

Jason faced forward. The judge gave his verdict.

"I find the accused not guilty—"

A wave of gasps erupted throughout the room. Jason tried to contain his excitement, but he felt like his heart skipped a beat.

"What the hell are you talking about?" Sheriff Townsend jumped from his seat. "How can you let that murdering bastard go free?"

The judge grabbed his gavel and pounded on his podium repeatedly until the room quieted.

"I will have order in this courtroom!" He pointed a gnarled, bony finger at Sheriff Townsend. "Any more outbursts like that, Sheriff, and you'll be the next man visiting the chair of the accused. Now. Sit. Down."

Townsend glared at the judge but finally conceded and sat down. Jason glanced at him and didn't try to keep the look of satisfaction from his face. The judge had found sufficient doubt and saw through Townsend's lies about the unarmed deputy.

Jason was free.

"Now, as I was saying," the judge said calmly. Jason fidgeted as he waited. "I find the accused not guilty on twenty-five counts of murder."

Jason's eyes narrowed.

"However, the defense presented no significant evidence to dispute the charge that the accused did, in fact, shoot and kill the deputy, and the prosecution presented evidence from a witness. On one count of the murder of Deputy Ross Billingsworth of Malden, Missouri, I regret finding the accused guilty as charged. At eight o'clock tomorrow morning, Jason Peares shall be hanged by the neck until he is dead."

CHAPTER 30

THE JUDGE POUNDED HIS GAVEL one final time, then rose and left the room. Stunned, Jason couldn't move. Shadows moved forward, and he felt hands grabbing his manacled arms. Strong hands forced him to stand, then guided him out the side door of the courthouse. Everything around him seemed like a blur as the armed guards half-dragged him down a side street toward the jail beyond the east edge of town.

Hours later in his cell, he listened to the hammering of the gallows outside the jail. He accepted the fact that he would die just after sunrise.

He'd always wondered how he would face death. He'd hoped to go down in a blaze of glorious gunfire. He always thought it would be quick and painless, maybe even heroic and exciting. He had hoped his death would somehow have purpose and meaning. He'd hoped to meet his maker saving someone who needed saving, not swinging at the end of a rope.

Jason always knew death would come sooner rather than later. As much as he wanted to deny the fact, he lived by his guns. There was no reason he should expect not to die the same way, directly or indirectly.

As things turned out, Renée could have been his salvation. She would have helped him put his guns away and begin a real life on a farm in California where no one would ever have found him.

The Santa Fe sheriff, Pickett was his name, had confiscated

everything in his pockets, including the letter Bonnie had given him. The letter had been written by Renée and sent to Bonnie from Greenville. He'd memorized it and read it over and over again in his mind.

Dearest Bonnie,

I was assigned to get Jason's confession, and I've heard it. But he's not the murderer we thought. I don't believe he killed that deputy, but I can't prove it without finding a witness to the first shooting. He's a good man, and so I've fallen in love with him. I'm resigning from the agency, and we're going to be married soon. I hope you won't think terrible of me. Please don't try to find me.

Your loving sister,

Shelley.

Jason smiled in the darkness, comforted by the thought that Renée really had loved him. He fell asleep on the cold floor, thinking about a life that might have been.

Sheriff Pickett, a tall, slender, serious man, came for him only minutes before eight o'clock. He chained Jason's ankles again and shackled his wrists behind his back. Solemnly, the sheriff escorted him into the front office. He was mildly annoyed that he wasn't even offered a last meal

Jason ambled along slowly, dragging his chains noisily between his boots. Four other quiet men stood leaning against walls in the room. The sneering Sheriff Townsend watched as Pickett led Jason toward the door. They walked out into the sunlight and through the walled courtyard where the gallows stood.

The silent crowd parted for the group, and the sheriff walked him up the steps to the platform, holding his arm to keep him from stumbling over his chains. Jason found the gesture amusing. He'd heard about some poor bastard over in Arizona who fell off the platform and broke a leg and an arm. The sheriff had to delay the hanging for three hours while a doctor set his limbs well enough so they could finally kill him.

Townsend stood beside the structure, close to the lever that would unlatch the shaky platform door. The three other guards moved a short distance away from the platform. Jason looked down at the trap door and hesitated, wondering if it would hold his weight. Suddenly, he didn't want to fall without the rope around his neck.

Sheriff Pickett gently nudged him forward. He checked the knots of the noose, then nudged Jason again to turn and face the crowd. Jason ducked his head slightly so the sheriff could easily fit the noose over his head and around his neck. The sheriff nodded his gratitude, but Jason said nothing. He just saw no point in being uncooperative.

He saw many familiar faces in the crowd below him. Many of the other prisoners he'd freed from the raiders came to watch. Some cried and others nodded or smiled when he looked at them.

Understanding? Gratitude? Farewell? He couldn't tell.

Jason thought of Sheriff Pickett as a decent man, even though the lawman was getting ready to kill him. Before affixing the noose, he had offered Jason a drink of water and a priest to prepare him for his journey to the hereafter, or wherever he was going. Jason had refused all of that.

He searched the crowd for Bonnie Drake. He didn't know exactly why he needed to see her. He thought maybe she'd at least stop by to wave goodbye or something. He let his gaze drift skyward as Sheriff Pickett began his formal rhetoric listing Jason's crime and punishment. He finished and looked up at Jason.

"Does the convicted have anything to say?"

Jason looked into the distance. "No."

As with most sizable towns Jason had passed through, Santa Fe's jail building sat past the edge of town, probably for safety if an inmate escaped. This particular jail sat about a quarter-mile east of town.

To his left, the east, Jason saw only mountains. To the south and west, beyond the earth-colored adobe buildings and shacks of the town, lay empty desert and more distant mountains. A movement in his side vision caught his attention. A shadow moved atop the flat roof of the church, beside the bell tower.

He spied his friend, the Arapaho warrior. The man held his bow by his side, unready. Jason looked at the man awhile, then he smiled and nodded with a single down-up movement of his head. He hoped the gesture conveyed his gratitude for the brief friendship they had shared.

The Indian looked away to the south, and Jason followed his gaze. A coach driver worked his horses hard in some kind of a hurry, likely for someone who didn't want to miss the hanging. He saw a puff of smoke from the driver's rifle, then heard the report several seconds later.

The lawmen around the hanging platform all turned at the sound, weapons ready. The crowd stepped aside as the guards moved to the edge of the jailhouse courtyard. The wagon raced around the south side of town and angled toward the low adobe wall. Then the driver did the unthinkable. He yanked on his reins and slammed the brake lever forward with the horses running full speed.

The animals protested loudly. Even before the coach came to a complete halt, the driver jumped down and hurriedly opened the door. Bonnie Drake ignored the driver's outstretched hand and leaped to the ground. She caught the front edge of her brown dress under her foot and stumbled forward, almost falling. Regaining her balance, she hurried through the open gate and ran over to the sheriff, lifting the front of her dress so she wouldn't stumble again.

"Sheriff, you cannot hang this man."

"Who are you?" Pickett asked quietly.

"Bonnie Drake, formerly of the Pinkerton National Detective Agency."

"I'm sorry, ma'am, but he's been tried and convicted."

"I know he was charged with many crimes, but I have a witness to the first shooting. I can prove he's not guilty of the original charge of murder. Maybe the judge will reconsider the other charges."

Pickett narrowed his eyes. "Miss Drake, all the other charges were dismissed."

Bonnie sucked in a gasp and looked up at Jason. "Oh, my God." She grabbed the front of Pickett's shirt. "You have to get the judge to reconsider."

Townsend stepped forward. "He's had his trial, lady. He's guilty, and now he's gonna die."

Sheriff Pickett was silent for a second, unsure of how to handle the situation. Finally, he noticed a second woman who had dismounted from the stagecoach. The woman walked up beside Bonnie.

"Sheriff, I was standing on the boardwalk that night when those men picked a fight with Jason. I'm lucky I didn't get shot with all the lead flying that night. So are a number of other people."

"He shot my deputy," Townsend bellowed. "I have witnesses!"

The woman turned to face Townsend. "He did no such thing. No one else was killed that night, and you know it."

Townsend looked sideways at Pickett, then shouted at the woman. "Who the hell are you anyway?"

"I am Melissa-Rae Hampton." She looked from Townsend to Pickett. "My husband was there also. He can testify if my word is not enough."

"The senator?" asked Pickett.

She nodded. "John Worthington Hampton."

Jason watched the exchange below him, confused as anyone. Like most folks, he knew of Senator Hampton—a powerful man who demanded attention. A smart sheriff didn't dismiss the word of his wife, either.

The sheriff removed his hat and ran a hand through his graying hair. He looked around at the crowd and stuck the hat back on his head. Jason would have bet a pouch of gold that Pickett was thinking about the judge's doubts about Townsend's evidence. Sheriff Townsend stood a few steps back, seething in anger.

Mrs. Hampton put her hands on her hips. "This sheriff came running to see this young man," Mrs. Hampton pointed at Jason, "standing over four dead men. He never even asked anyone what happened. Jason Peares had already thrown down both his guns. He was unarmed when the sheriff got there. He simply dragged that poor young man off to jail."

The sheriff narrowed his eyes. "This man didn't shoot an unarmed deputy?"

Melissa-Rae Hampton shook her head and looked at Sheriff Townshend. "There was no deputy around. Just him." She pointed at Townsend.

Pickett took a deep breath. He nodded to one of his guards and motioned his hand at Jason.

"All right, get him down from there." To Mrs. Hampton he said, "The judge will want to hear your testimony and ask you some questions."

Mrs. Hampton screamed, and the sheriff turned. Jason looked down as Townsend launched his massive frame toward the structure. He reached for the drop lever.

Jason sucked in his breath and tensed his entire body. But he didn't fall. Sheriff Pickett held his gun pointed at the side of Townsend's head.

"You'll die with him, Sheriff."

"You gonna shoot me and let this bastard go free?"

"I ain't gonna shoot you unless you pull that handle, mister," Pickett said. "Now step back. Let's do this the right way."

Townsend looked from Pickett to the drop lever, and then to the gun at his head. He nodded and withdrew his hand, then stepped back and turned away. He looked up and gave Jason a wicked smile that Pickett didn't see.

Sheriff Pickett reached for Townsend's arm and had just started to lower his gun when Townsend spun around and slammed his fist into Pickett's face. The Santa Fe sheriff fell back and sprawled in the dirt. Bonnie Drake started forward, but she was too far away to stop Townsend. The guards, who had relocated at the approach of the stagecoach, were blocked by the crowd.

Townsend reached out, still looking up at Jason. Still sneering, he pulled the drop lever and Jason fell.

CHAPTER 31

T HE TRAP DOOR DROPPED UNDER Jason's weight. He felt
the free fall for barely a second before the rope tightened
around his neck. He held his breath and clenched his
eyes shut. The end had finally come. Sheriff Townsend had won.
The man had traveled across half the states to watch him fall.

Then Jason hit the ground on his rump, and when he opened
his eyes, he saw Townsend's face gaping at him. The sheriff
looked up in disbelief, and Jason followed the sheriff's gaze.
They both stared up through the trap door opening and saw an
arrow stuck deep in one of the wooden supports of the platform.
The warrior's obsidian arrowhead had sliced clean through the
rope, fired from a hundred yards away!

Townsend cursed like a madman and pulled his gun. He
almost had it pointed at Jason's head when he stumbled sideways. His eyes widened as he looked down. For a moment, he
stared at the arrowhead sticking out of the front of his shirt, just
below his badge. He had a look of shock—sheer disbelief—on
his face. It was one of the nasty ones, Jason noticed. The wicked
arrowhead had pounded all the way through the man's thick
chest and protruded from his body with bits of flesh still stuck
to it. Townsend's eyes glazed in shock, but he still brought the
gun up. Then he jerked again as another arrow slammed into
him. Townsend howled in pain and fell to his knees. He managed to bring the gun all the way up and still looked at Jason
with murder in his eyes. Jason rolled toward him, pivoting on

his right hip. He lashed out at the gun with his chained legs as the gun discharged and a third arrow thumped into Townsend's torso. Jason's boots caught the sheriff on his right shoulder and knocked the gun aside just as Townsend fired a second time.

Jason felt the hot powder burn the left side of his face. The bullet kicked up dirt that stung his eyes, and the explosion of sound deafened him. He saw a shadow of movement as he blinked, thought he saw Townsend fall over. A flash of light glinted nearby, and Jason rolled onto it. It was the gun Sheriff Pickett had dropped to catch his balance. Hands still chained behind his back and still linked to the shackles on his ankles, Jason felt for the gun under him. The sheriff clawed at him and climbed up his body. He grabbed Jason's pants, his shirt, his belt, whatever he could get his hands on. Then he wrapped first one big beefy hand, then another, around his neck. He squeezed tightly with incredible strength for a man so gravely wounded.

Jason searched frantically for the gun. He managed to touch it twice, but he kept knocking it away. He couldn't get a grip on it, and the sheriff's strong hands steadily cut off his air supply. Darkness closed in at the edges of his blurred vision. He couldn't breathe, couldn't fight any longer, and he felt consciousness slipping away. Then, suddenly, he had the gun in his grasp.

Jason fumbled with the gun in hands still chained behind his back and almost dropped it. He contorted his body, brought his hands around to his side as much as the chains would allow, and then pulled the trigger as fast as he could. But the grip around his neck didn't diminish. He must have missed, must have shot everything except Townsend. He heard the sheriff growling in his ear, felt the man pressing him into the dirt, killing him.

Then the pressure around his neck was gone, as the sheriff expelled his final breath and collapsed on top of Jason. He felt the sharp arrowhead scratching his chest as he struggled to get out from under the dead man. People nearby pulled the man aside, and Jason gasped, filling his lungs with air in case he never got the chance again. He felt hands at his neck loosening the noose and removing the coarse rope. He blinked several times to clear his vision and saw a brown dress.

Bonnie Drake rolled him into her lap and helped him sit up. His left ear still throbbed, and he had to twist his head to hear her speak in his other ear. The left side of his face felt scratched and raw. His neck hurt when he swallowed, bruised by the rope that almost yanked his head from his shoulders and then by Townsend's grip.

With Bonnie's help, Jason finally stood shakily after he caught his breath. Sheriff Townsend lay nearby on his side. Four gunshot wounds, all placed in a space the size of a fist, bloodied the front of his shirt. Three thick arrow shafts stuck out his back and his side.

Jason looked toward the church but saw no sign of the Indian. *Damn good shooting,* he thought, *from a hundred yards away.*

Sheriff Pickett recovered, helped up by his deputies, and led Jason back into the jail. The next day, he personally escorted Jason out into the courtyard and handed him five signed copies of warrants announcing his freedom. Jason took the papers and smiled as he shook the sheriff's hand.

"I just hope whoever ain't got the word yet can read," Jason said.

The sheriff chuckled and nodded to the gate. Bonnie Drake waited with Jason's horse and pack. They walked the short distance to town, leading their horses. She seemed to know his thoughts.

"When I left you near Rattler's Bend, I resigned from the Pinkertons and went back to Malden to find the witness. Shelley...I mean, Renée.... She would've wanted that."

Jason nodded. "I thought that would've been the first place your detectives visited when you first took after me last year."

"Of course. But at that time, we had no reason to doubt Sheriff Townsend's word. We had no reason to look for witnesses for you. You were already guilty as far as we were concerned. We didn't think to check his signed statements." She paused.

"It never occurred to us that the sheriff had such a...personal hatred for you."

Jason nodded. "I defied him. He told me back then that no White men would hang on the word of a Black kid, and then I went and killed them. I guess he took that kinda personal."

Bonnie nodded and continued. "Well, this time I couldn't track down any witnesses, but I heard about a saloon girl named Donna who lived in Malden seven years ago. She was mentioned in a report as a person you'd been seen with then. I found her and her parents living down in Texas. Her mother, Mrs. Hampton, agreed to testify."

"You did all that in six weeks? That's a lot of riding."

Bonnie socked him firmly on the shoulder and gave him a look that called him stupid. "I took the train, silly!"

Jason smiled. "I knew that."

He felt comfortable walking beside Bonnie. Everyone he passed stared at him, but he didn't mind. For the first time in his adult life, he could walk through a town in broad daylight. He was free, no longer an outlaw. He'd live on the trail now only if he wanted to.

Bonnie told him he could find Mrs. Hampton at the hotel. He tied up his horse, and Bonnie went into the general store while Jason walked into the hotel lobby.

Mrs. Hampton stood about five feet tall, a full-figured woman. She wore a dark blue, high-necked dress. A delicate string of exquisite jewels shimmered around her neck. She had her gray hair pinned up under an elegant, wide-brimmed blue hat.

"I owe you my life, Mrs. Hampton."

"Please, call me Melissa-Rae. And you're very welcome." She smiled again, the barest hint of wrinkles creasing the edges of her eyes.

"Yes, ma'am," said Jason. "But I'm afraid you got some details of your story wrong."

She smiled conspiratorially and looked away. "Really?"

"Yes, ma'am. Nowadays, I'm known to wear a two-gun rig, but back then I only had one gun. And I didn't throw it down like you said. The sheriff snatched it from me and smacked me upside the head with it before shoving me down in the street. Townsend ground my face in the mud while he put chains on me. Then he dragged me off to jail."

"I'm afraid my daughter didn't have much time to help me get my story straight," Melissa-Rae said. "That sheriff found out she was the only person who knew your name back then. He threatened to kill her if she didn't tell him. I figure if a sheriff can threaten people and fabricate a lie to make you a criminal, then I can tell a small fib to give you back your freedom."

"Melissa-Rae," Jason said, reaching for her hand. "If you ever need anything," he paused. "Anything at all, you just call on me. Anytime, anywhere." He kissed the back of her hand on the soft flesh near the knuckle.

Melissa-Rae nodded and turned away. Jason left the hotel and looked to his left. He caught Bonnie's gaze as she walked toward him. She smiled and, for a brief moment, he saw Renée's eyes again. Then, the illusion vanished and he saw Bonnie again.

Jason pivoted and took his first step toward Bonnie. He heard the familiar metallic sound of danger just before his boot heel hit the boardwalk.

CHAPTER 32

BONNIE LOOKED AT HIM, STILL smiling, but her eyes darted to her left, distracted by a movement in the street. Jason's brain immediately identified the metallic sound. Someone had rammed a rifle lever forward and back, chambering a cartridge. His heart pounded an extra beat. He felt the wild rush of adrenaline galvanize his body into action.

Bonnie's eyes opened wide in surprise, and her mouth opened as she started to shout a warning, all in the tiny instant of time that Jason's boot touched the boardwalk. There was no time to look at the danger and identify it. The knowledge that danger was close was enough of a motivation. Instinctively, Jason ducked, found himself sheltered behind a horse tied at the hitching rail. The rifle barked with the deep throaty explosion of a large-bore buffalo gun.

Faster than Jason could react, the bullet exploded through the hind quarter of the horse. He felt the wind of the bullet flash by the tip of his nose. Barely an instant later, the bullet thumped into the wall to his left, exploding splinters into the air.

Blood and gore from the horse's wound splattered over the side of Jason's face. The horse's hindquarter slammed into him, launching him airborne against the wall. He bounced off hard and was dazed. Trying to keep his balance, he stumbled over the fallen animal as it kicked in the throes of death.

Jason scrambled on his hands and feet until he regained his balance. In midstride, he slapped his palm against his thigh, reaching for a nonexistent holster gun. He spun and rolled, then jumped up, running again.

The second bullet hit the thick wooden lamppost beside him. The ricochet ahead of Jason gouged a chunk of wood out of the wall. He saw Bonnie trying to get a shot, but surprised people stood in her way. Jason hollered, reached out. She tossed her gun at him.

He caught the pistol in a rolling dive and fired just as the shooter locked down his third round. His shot scored high in the left side of the old man's chest. He staggered back a step, then sagged to his knees.

He raised the rifle again, shouting at Jason, his dark eyes filled with hatred. "You gots to kill me like you done my boys!"

The man started to aim, and Jason fired again. His bullet struck the man in the chest barely an inch from the first. The old man jerked and dropped the rifle. He glared at Jason for a few seconds, then he fell over sideways.

Jason used his sleeve to wipe the horse's blood and gore from the side of his face. Bonnie stepped up beside Jason and touched his shoulder gently. She walked with him into the street, toward the dead man. A few minutes later, Sheriff Pickett and two deputies rode up and dismounted.

"What happened here?"

"That fellow took the first shot at this 'n," someone said, gesturing toward Jason.

"From the backside, no less," said another.

Jason gave Bonnie back her gun. "He said I killed his boys, Sheriff."

"You know this man?" the sheriff said.

Jason shook his head. "Not that I recall."

Sheriff Pickett turned to examine the dead man and his weapon.

Bonnie nodded at the buffalo gun. "That there's a .56-caliber Sharps, if I'm not mistaken."

"Yeah, it's a big one," Jason said nodding. "Bullet went

through that horse like it wasn't even there." He nodded over to the boardwalk.

She agreed. "I've seen hunters take down two, sometimes three buffalo at 600 yards with a single shot from one of those guns."

"He missed me by the skin on my nose."

Bonnie looked at him. "It was that close?"

He nodded. "I felt the wind of that big bullet go right by my face. If it had even grazed me, there wouldn't have been enough of my head left to recognize me."

"Let me buy you a drink," Bonnie said. "There's a quiet place on the north edge of town. Over next to the feed store."

He nodded, and they walked over to get their horses. Jason glanced around continually as he unpacked his holsters and guns. The reality hit him quickly. He would still have to live by his guns. He had no choice in the matter.

Bonnie Drake watched him with a concerned look on her face. He ignored her. He just strapped on his gun belt and tied the leg straps. Then, he checked the chambers of both his Schofield holster guns and tested them for ease of the fast draw like he'd done a thousand times over the years. Except back then he'd been an outlaw. Now, he was a free man, but he knew that detail wouldn't matter to the men still hunting him. He unpacked his Colt .45s and stuck them in his belt, butts facing outward for the easy grab. He wiped his face clean with a kerchief and put on a clean shirt in the middle of the street.

"Sheriff," Jason called. He reached into his back pocket and pulled out his freedom papers and tossed them into the street. "Looks like I didn't get the chance to ask him if he could read."

The sheriff nodded. "I reckon he wouldn't have cared much anyway. Good luck to you, son."

Jason walked with Bonnie, leading his horse through the streets of town. As they headed toward the saloon on the north side, he kept his eyes moving. He scrutinized everything and everyone, constantly searching for danger. He tied up his horse at the post, then took another look around. He retrieved some coins from a saddlebag and pocketed them.

Jason and Bonnie went into the empty saloon and stepped over to the bar on the left side of the room. The barkeep slept in a chair at the back with his feet propped up on a table. An open bottle of whiskey sat on the bar next to some dusty glasses. Jason placed a coin on the bar, blew powdery dirt out of two glasses, and poured their drinks.

Bonnie nodded her gratitude and raised her glass to his. She looked at him over her drink. Jason found himself staring into Renée's eyes again.

"Do you believe in fate, Bonnie? In God?"

"Yes." She hesitated, then added, "Do you?"

"In truth, I've never had much use for the Almighty." He sipped his whiskey. "But sometimes I wonder if things happen for a reason." He took a deep breath and thought for a moment.

"I feel responsible for my sister's death, Jason. I should have done like she asked and stayed away."

Jason nodded. "You didn't really believe she wrote that letter, did you? Maybe you thought I wrote it and had killed her, or was keeping her prisoner or something."

Bonnie said, "If I hadn't come looking for her, she'd still be alive."

"And I'd still be a wanted man," he finished. "Sure, maybe we would've gone off to California and lived comfortable for a while. We might even have gotten married like we planned and had a family. But more likely, it was just a matter of time before someone found me and ended it. She might have been close to me when it happened." He took a deep breath. "A lot of people close to me at the wrong time end up dead."

Jason reached for Bonnie's hand. "Outlaw life has only one ending. Her letter sent you to find a witness that saved my life. And her words to Miss Constance Morgan accounted for me saving a lot of people, Bonnie. Almost fifty people still live who most certainly would have died otherwise."

Bonnie nodded and closed her eyes for a moment.

Jason said, "Because of your sister's sacrifice, we've been able to do good by a lot of people, you and me."

They both stood silently for a long time, absently sipping on their drinks.

"I'll be leaving soon," Jason said softly.

"I know." She looked at him suggestively with a look that he'd seen before. "Maybe we could ride together for a while." She chuckled and brought out her saloon girl personality and accent he'd first heard in Salina, so many months past. "Good women are hard to find out on the frontier, especially for good men."

He shook his head slowly. "Except I'm not one of the good men, Bonnie. Not after what I did to all those outlaws."

Even though Cordova and Masters and all the rest were very bad men, he still shuddered as he recalled how he had dispatched them without remorse and without regard to any law. He hadn't felt good about what he'd done, but he had wanted to feel good. He wanted it to be a gratifying, vengeful experience. Now that he knew he was capable of killing men for revenge, he also knew it would be easier the next time.

"I think you are one of the good men," she said. "It would've been nice to get to know you better."

"You're different from her. Different from how I figured you to be when we met in Salina. But trouble comes to visit me far too often."

Bonnie nodded at the dirt street beyond the wall. "Maybe that old man came all the way from who-knows-where just to see you hang."

"How many other kinfolk are out there looking for me? Waiting to shoot me in the back because I killed their kin some time ago? They won't care if I'm an outlaw or not. When people hear I didn't hang, they'll start here to pick up my trail."

"Where are you going to go?"

He waved an arm at the opposite wall, indicating the expanse of desert beyond.

"Out there, where innocent people like you can't catch any

bullets for me." He paused. "I'm going to ride with the warrior for a while. I reckon I have something to prove to him now."

He gazed into her eyes, then stepped forward and hugged her tight. He held her for a long time. When he stepped back, he saw Renée's eyes. He held her close again. He found himself wondering where she'd go and how she would deal with the loss of a sister.

Behind him the saloon door swung open on squeaky hinges. He heard a pair of boots stomp in two paces. Glancing over his shoulder, Jason saw a familiar face. It was Stanley Comb, the young gunfighter from Franklin Town.

"Jason Peares, I'm callin' you out!"

Jason nudged Bonnie Drake away from him. Then he turned to face Comb.

"You come all the way out here to New Mexico just to get killed, kid?" Jason began the mental battle with his opponent.

"I can take you."

Stanley Comb stared at him, his wild blue eyes betraying his excitement and fear. Jason waited a few more seconds, but the kid made no move.

"Well," Jason said. "Are you gonna take me…today…or are you going to wait, maybe until I fall asleep?"

"I can take you," the young gunfighter repeated. His voice cracked.

Stanley Comb drew his gun.

Almost.

TO BE CONTINUED

If you enjoyed this adventure, check out the next book in the Jason Peares saga at JeffreyPostonBooks.com or wherever you buy books. Please let other readers know what you thought of the book by leaving a brief review at your favorite retailer. It only takes a moment and reviews are very valuable to authors.

THE MAKING OF COURAGE

Courage is chronologically the first in the four-book Jason Peares historical western series, but I actually wrote it last. I envisioned this story as the "origins" novel—where Jason Peares came from and how he became the outlaw gunfighter he is. At the same time, I wanted to push the boundaries of the traditional western a bit.

So in this story, I pitted our hero against a very capable and deadly frontier detective...that was a woman!

This is a work of fiction, but the origins and expansion of the Pinkerton National Detective Agency in the early 1880s was very real and well documented in the history books. Did you know that the Pinkerton Agency women were some of its most accomplished "cowboy detectives?" Indeed, these cowgirl detectives were every bit as trained and capable as their male counterparts. It is reported that some could handle firearms as well as men and female sharpshooters could hit the belly button on a snake at two hundred yards! Well, that is, if snakes actually had belly buttons.

What I've tried to capture in this story are the thoughts and feelings and fears of a wanted man pursued by detectives of a professional man-hunting agency, all the while dreaming of love and family and of a time and place where he might live free from pursuit.

ABOUT THE AUTHOR

Jeffrey Poston is the acclaimed author of the Jason Peares historical western series, as well as the fast-paced adventure thriller series *American Terrorist* and *Call Sign: Raven*. Blending traditional and revisionist historical research, his historical westerns have been praised as "fast-moving" (Kelton) and "exciting, page-turning" (Zollinger) and "among the best writers of westerns" (Biblio.com). His thriller books are lauded as "so realistic," "powerfully intense," and "action-packed page turners." He is a self-described *Rambling Man* and writes his novels wherever he happens to be in his travels.

Find Jeffrey at http://www.jeffreypostonbooks.com/

Amazon.com: http://amazon.com/author/jeffreyposton

Facebook: http://www.facebook.com/JeffreyPostonBooks

Twitter: http://www.twitter.com/BooksByJPoston

Goodreads: http://www.goodreads.com/JeffreyPoston

ACKNOWLEDGMENTS

As writers, we often go into our creative caves to compose a book, but when we come out, there are often dozens of people who help refine a story and turn it into a really good book. No writer can succeed without this special group of people—critical readers, cover artists, professional editors, marketing and PR specialists, and publishers.

I especially want to thank my critical reader and sounding board, Dr. Stephanie McIver. She's helped me through many of my books, offering insight and analysis that added depth and breadth to my characters and my plot.

Special thanks to Debra L. Hartmann, The Pro Book Editor, and her team for copyediting and proofreading. I also want to give a shout-out to the cover art designers of my books: Deanna Dionne.

I'm also thankful for the active imaginations (and the suspension of disbelief) of all the readers who enjoyed my Western and Thriller adventures. I'm especially grateful to the dozens of beta-readers who previewed the book and sent back invaluable advice. Your help means the world to this author!